PRAISE FOR MARI MANCUSI AND *SK8ER BOY*!

"A funny, touching story about the guy a girl never knew she wanted. I loved it!"
—Bestselling author Niki Burnham

"A great book for every good girl who ever wondered what it would be like to be just a little bit bad. Mari Mancusi is a fresh and edgy new talent in teen and tween fiction."
—Jax Abbott, author of *Super 16*

KISS IT BETTER

"You're bleeding," I say, kneeling down to check Sean's battle wound—a big bloody raspberry. "I may have a Band-Aid in my purse…"

He laughs. "My little Florence Nightingale," he teases. "I don't need a Band-Aid. I just need you to kiss it better."

I look down at the bloody mess on his knee. "You want me to kiss…that?" I ask, a little hesitantly. I mean, I like the guy and all, but eewwhh.

He cracks up and takes my head in his hands. "No, silly. I hurt my lips."

SK8ER BOY

Mari Mancusi

SMOOCH NEW YORK CITY

To all the real life "Sk8er Boys"
I have known and loved…

SMOOCH ®

October 2005

Published by

Dorchester Publishing Co., Inc.
200 Madison Avenue
New York, NY 10016

ISBN 0-8439-5604-6

The name "SMOOCH" and its logo are trademarks of Dorchester Publishing Co., Inc.

Printed in the United States of America.

Visit us on the web at www.smoochya.com.

SK8ER BOY

Chapter One

"Hey, Dawn, whatcha writing?"

I slam my notebook shut and force a wide smile as my friend Ashley approaches the lunch table. I can't believe it. She's five minutes early. Five minutes! After I've already gone and used up one of my three-bathroom-breaks-a-semester chemistry class privileges for a few precious moments of writing time. And now Ashley has shown up and ruined it all.

The early bird gets the chance to tick Dawn off. . . .

"Nothing," I say, forcing a casual shrug. "Just a birthday wish list. You know how The Evil Ones are. Left to their own devices I'd probably end up with some itchy Harvard letter sweater for my sweet sixteen."

I'd actually been working on a poem, not a birthday list. One I plan to enter in a contest sponsored by *Faces*, a local Massachusetts literary magazine. But I am certainly not about to inform our head cheerleader of that little technicality. I mean, writing poetry? How geeky can you get? And The Evil Ones (aka Mom and Dad) *are* terrible in the presents department, so it's not like I'm telling a total lie. . . .

"Oh cool." Ashley flounces onto the chair beside me, her wool plaid skirt puffing up and then settling back down over her perfectly sculpted thighs. We all wear the same skirts here as sophomores at Sacred Mary's—little Britney Spears clones, the lot of us. But Ashley's skirt usually falls at least two inches shorter than regulation and it constantly gets her in trouble with the Sisters. "You should ask for those Seven Jeans we saw at Jasmine Sola the other day."

"The ones with the crystals on the back pocket?" I look up and see that Ashley #2 has arrived at our lunch table. Like Ashley #1, she's blond and lanky and wears her skirts too short. Her claim to fame is being picked as homecoming queen last fall, even though she's only a sophomore. "Those are completely lame. When shopping for jeans, I say go James every time. They're scientifically designed to make your butt look smaller, not draw attention to it with crystals."

I stifle a groan. I love my friends, don't get me wrong. But there are times I'm not quite sure I fit in with them. I mean yeah, I'd rather be here than at the loser table discussing games like Magic: The Gathering, but is it really necessary for us to debate the pros and cons of designer denim every single lunch? Doesn't anyone talk politics anymore? Not that I know anything about politics, but maybe I could start learning if someone brought them up once in a while. It'd probably prove more useful in life than the Fashionista 101 sessions we seem to hold every lunch period.

"You guys are crazy!" Oh, there's Ashley #3, making our lunch group complete. She swings her Kate Spade messenger bag off her shoulder and plops it on the floor. We consider Ashley #3 the brainy one. She's president of the student council and wants to be a TV anchorwoman when she grows up. I think she has a good shot at the job. She's already got the brilliant white capped teeth and perfect hair. "Obviously Levi's makes the best jeans known to mankind."

The other two Ashleys groan in sync. "No way would I be caught dead in Levi's," says Ashley #1.

"That's 'cause you're a lemming," Ashley #3 explains, using the big word with a smug pride. She knows for a fact Ashley #1 won't know what it means and she's right.

"Hey! What did you just call me?"

"Girls, girls! Let us not fight over fashion," Ashley #2, the peacemaker, coos. She took a yoga class once and has been all Buddha-on-the-mountain ever since. "Our different tastes in denim make the world go round." She holds her palms out and smiles demurely. For a minute I think she's going to actually break out into an "Ohmmm."

Instead she says, "What were we talking about again?"

"Dawn's birthday wish list."

"Ah. How about a side of Brent Baker, served on a silver platter?" Her demure smile morphs into a lecherous smirk as she watches the senior from across the room. We all turn and look. The Ashleys sigh, again in sync. They're good at that.

"No way. He's on *my* birthday list," declares Ashley #1. This obviously strikes them as funny, and all three break out into giggles.

You know, I'm pretty convinced I'm the only girl in school not lusting after Brent Baker. Brent Baker the Third, that is. Born with a silver spoon wedged up his butt. His parents and my parents go to the same country club, so I've known him since my playpen days and he's been after me almost as long. But I'm soooo not interested in him. I mean, sure he's got the blond, blue-eyed jock thing going on, but his huge ego negates any points he's chocked up in the looks department.

The Ashleys can't understand why I think he's repulsive, but they don't rock the boat. After all, that means he's fair game for any one of them.

"Hi, Brent," coos Ashley #1 as the varsity football player approaches our table. He's all Abercrombie'd out, as usual. (Seniors at Sacred Mary's have the luxury of forgoing uniforms, as long as they don't abuse the privilege with Von Dutch trucker hats and low, low, butt-crack-revealing jeans.)

"Ladies," he greets, offering a smarmy grin. I resist the urge to roll my eyes. "Dawn," he adds, coming behind me and placing his hands on my shoulders. I shrug away. I usually try to be civil to him—The Evil Ones would kill me if I weren't—but I draw the line at shoulder massages.

"Hi, Brent," I mutter.

"Did you hear about the new girl?" he asks, plopping down beside me. I slide as far as I can to the other side of my stool. Brent always reeks of too much cologne and it makes my eyes water. Or maybe I'm just allergic to cheesiness.

The Ashleys lean in, eager for the gossip. "What new girl?" questions Ashley #3, honing her journalistic skills.

"Well," Brent says in a conspiratorial voice. He's delighted he's gotten our full attention. Pathetic. "Supposedly she's the headmaster's daughter. And I heard she got kicked out of boarding school for being part of a satanic cult."

"Oh, her!" Ashley #1 exclaims, as if previously thrown off by the masses of new students Sacred Mary's has acquired in the last week. She bobs her head in all-knowingness. "I heard from a very reliable source that she's a witch. And she drinks the blood of snakes after cutting off their heads."

I know for a fact Ashley's "very reliable source" is her on-again, off-again boyfriend Derek. Who is not reliable at all, IMO.

"Ri-ight," I say sarcastically. "And she eats babies for breakfast, too."

"Really? Wow!" Ashley #1 looks impressed. "I hadn't heard that part."

Sigh. Just sigh.

"Ooh! Look! Is that her?" Ashley #2 exclaims with a squeak. I follow her pointing finger to a girl who has just exited the lunch line, tray in hand, and a slightly defiant look on her face.

"Oh my gosh, she looks like Marilyn Manson!" Ashley #3 whispers so loudly that I'm almost convinced the new girl can hear her from across the caf.

"No she doesn't," I hiss back, a lot more quietly. "She's pretty. She looks like the girl from Evanescence."

She does look a lot like Amy Lee, I decide, as I take another peek. What with her long, jet-black hair and powder-white skin. She's wearing a black zippered hoodie over her uniform top and has rolled her regulation Catholic-schoolgirl skirt down to reveal an inch of stomach skin. I'm surprised none of the Ashleys have ever tried that look before. On her feet she's wearing black combat boots. (Not surprised they skipped that trend. It's pointy-toed shoes or die with the Ashleys.)

The nuns are going to have a field day with this chick.

"Let's get her to come sit with us," I suggest, feeling a moment of compassion for the new girl. "She probably doesn't know anyone."

All three Ashleys and one Brent Baker the Third turn to stare at me, mouths agape.

"You're kidding, right? Puh-leeze tell me you're kidding," says Ashley #1.

"If you're not kidding, you must be blind. Do you see what she looks like?" That from Ashley #2. "She's a total skank."

"If we invite her over, we might as well invite all the other losers in the lunchroom. Want me to get the gamer geeks over to our table, Dawn? How about the drama dorks?" That's Ashley #3's contribution.

"Okay, fine. Sorry!" I say with a huff. "It was just a suggestion. Jeez."

Like I said, I love my friends, but I am aware they're truly the shallowest people on the planet. Like, they'd never even consider accepting anyone into their inner circle who doesn't embrace the color pink. And God help you if you have on the wrong shoes. At times, I'm surprised they include me in their little reindeer games. After all, strike one—I'm not even called Ashley. (Though it is my middle name.)

In any case, the four of us bonded long ago in elementary school (I had the best Barbie collection!) and I'm somehow still hanging around with them. And while they get on my nerves at times, it's better than having no friends at all. To be forced to sit by myself at lunch like the new girl. So I put up with them for the most part. And really, at times they can be fun. Especially when we're shopping.

I watch curiously as the supposed snake-blood-drinking witch-Satanist starts picking at her mystery meat. I feel bad for staring, but she's just so intriguing. Not like anyone I've ever seen at Sacred Mary's.

She doesn't seem to mind sitting by herself. In fact, she almost seems to glow with self-assurance. Like she doesn't care what others think of her. I wish I had half that confidence.

Abruptly, she turns around and catches me staring at her. She raises one eyebrow as she appraises me, then rolls her eyes and turns back to her food. I can feel my cheeks heat with embarrassment. In that one moment, it's as if she's weighed me and found me wanting. She thinks I'm exactly like my silly friends. Just another one of the blond, blue-eyed Ashley clones—all fluff and fashion and no substance. One of The Plastics. The Populars. The Mean Girls. Whatever tired movie cliché you want to use.

For some strange reason, I suddenly get the undying urge to prove her wrong.

Chapter Two

I arrive home at exactly 7:05 P.M. that evening and I no sooner drop my Marc Jacobs carryall on our foyer's marble floor, than The Evil Ones start in with their nightly game of Dawn harassment.

"How was school?" my mother asks from her seated position on the beige couch in our Victorian-themed parlor. I don't know how she and Dad can sit in there. Even the raging fire in the fireplace can't warm the icily formal room.

"School was fine. So was crew before school and gymnastics after. And yes, I got an A on my math test." I know they're going to badger me about each and every one of these activities, so I figure I might as well throw them all out on the table at once so we can move on.

"You know, I was looking at your schedule for next year," Dad pipes in from his armchair, after setting down the big fat book he's reading. "And I see you have a study scheduled in B period."

Shoot. I was hoping he wouldn't notice that. "Oh. Do I?" I ask, trying to sound innocent. I shift my weight onto my left foot and smooth down my pleated skirt as I wait for the condemnation to come.

"Don't you think it'd be better to sign up for AP History in that slot?"

I love how he pretends something's a question when it's so obviously a demand. As if I could actually say, "No, Dad, next semester I'd actually like a millisecond of free time" and he'd be okay with it.

"Most people don't take AP History 'til senior year, Dad," I say halfheartedly. I know I'll lose the argument. I always do. "I'll only be a junior."

"No reason why you can't get ahead. After all, Harvard doesn't accept slackers, you know."

I cringe. There he goes again with the "H" word. That's all he cares about. Harvard. His alma mater. The school he's determined that I get into. And to make sure I do, he's scheduled me within an inch of my life—with honors classes and extracurricular activities up the wazoo. He says I need to be well-rounded. At this point, I'm so round it's amazing I don't roll away.

I would love to tell him that I'm not interested in going to Harvard, that I'd rather go to some small liberal-arts school in California (far away from them!) to study poetry, but I'm afraid the revelation might kill him. After all, he's got that heart condition. My parents are on the older side, you see. Mom did the whole career thing before popping out a kid. That's why I never got a brother or sister. By the time I was born, her eggs had shriveled up.

"Okay, Dad. I'll sign up for AP History," I acquiesce. Better to appease him than doom myself to a half-hour lecture. "I'm, um, going up to my room now."

"Do you have homework?" Mom asks. Remember that career I mentioned she had? Teacher. And even in retirement, nothing school-related gets past her.

I suppress a sigh. "I'll do it in my room."

"I'd better not come up there and find you writing your little limericks," Dad warns, picking up his gigantic book again. Some obscure medieval text that no one in their right mind would read for pleasure. "After all, you've got to keep those grades up. Last semester, you got an A-minus in Biology and—"

"Okay, Dad. I won't write poetry. I'll study." I grab my bag off the floor and trudge upstairs to my room.

Limericks indeed. You know, no one appreciates my poetry. No one. But someday, when I'm a famous author, people are going to bid big money on eBay for these early verses. And I'll go on Oprah and talk about how my creativity was stifled at an early age. *"I'm so lucky to have made it through at all, Op,"* I'll say. (We'll have little pet names for each other at this point.) *"Well, the world is glad you did, Darla,"* she'll say, using my soon-to-be world-famous pen name. And then the talk-show host will bring out my old gray parents who will lament how wrong they were to hinder my creative genius, while the audience boos them off stage.

I hang a left at the top of the stairs and head down the hall to my bedroom. My sanctuary. The one place in this house where no one's allowed to bug me. Sure, it's still got the expensive, formal furniture, inherited from Grandma like everything else in this monstrosity of a mansion we call home, but I've softened the look with magazine cutouts of my favorite old movie stars on the walls. As I lie in bed at night, Audrey Hepburn and James Dean and Marilyn Monroe smile down at me, as if to tell me that everything will be okay.

I light an aromatherapy candle and plop, stomach down, onto my bed, taking a deep breath in an attempt to unwind. I'm only fifteen, but some days I'm convinced I'm on the verge of a mid-life crisis. I'm overscheduled, stressed to the max, and the caffeine's no longer working.

You know how normal kids go through their teen years? Wake up at seven, go to school, take some easy classes like basket-weaving or drama and then go hang with their friends and listen to music? Well, imagine my day. You're up at five to go to crew practice, rowing down a river in the freezing Massachusetts air. Change quickly to make it to school in time for the first bell. Then have a school day cram-packed with AP and honors classes. Last bell rings and you're off to gymnastics practice or yearbook or school paper or ballet or whatever and then straight to your language tutor where you're learning Japanese in case you want to be a foreign business leader someday (which you don't). You get home at seven o'clock and go up to your room to do all your excruciatingly hard AP and honors homework. Go to bed after homework is finished, then wake up the next morning to do it all again.

Basically, every second of my life is booked solid 'til I retire. (The Evil Ones have probably already pre-registered me for a nursing home, too.) Doesn't sound like fun? Too bad, 'cause I'd love to trade places with anyone who envies me.

I open my Algebra II textbook and my half-finished

poem flutters onto my bed. I glance over at my closed bedroom door. Will Dad really come up and check on me? The poetry contest deadline is tomorrow, and I have no idea when I'll be able to finish writing it if I don't do it tonight. And I really want to enter, too. The prize is a hundred dollars and publication in the magazine. Of course, I'd have to use a pen name, but that's okay. I'd know it was mine.

But just as I'm about to put pen to paper and become one with my writing muse, a knock sounds on my door. I groan and stuff the poem back into my Algebra book. So much for sanctuary.

"Come in."

My mother enters the room, all pearl necklaces and Chanel No. 5, as usual. Before she became an English teacher and mother to me, she was a fashion-magazine model, which is more than likely how she nabbed my rich, older father back in the day. Once when I was spying in her bedroom, I found her old modeling scrapbook stuffed in her underwear drawer. She was beautiful back then, I'll give her that. A smooth-skinned, dark-eyed Italian beauty. Very Sophia Loren. I bet she was super disappointed when I came out of her womb all Irish and freckled, like my dad.

She frowns disapprovingly at my sprawled-out position on the bed.

"You know, you have a very nice desk," she says, gesturing to the mahogany nightmare on the far left of my bedroom. Like I said, she was a model, so she's big on the whole posture thing.

"I sit at a desk all day, Mom." I tug on a blond braid in

frustration. Why can't she just leave me alone? I mean, what does it really matter whether I study on my bed or at a desk?

Her frown deepens, but she doesn't pursue the subject. "Well, I just came up to tell you that Magda should have dinner ready in about five minutes."

Magda, our housekeeper/cook, is from Mexico and makes the best meals known to mankind. Spicy Spanish dishes that deliciously burn my lips when I take a bite. The Evil Ones are constantly nagging her that she's going to give me heartburn and to make my meals milder, but I can usually convince her to add extra spice when they're not looking. Magda's cool like that. In fact, she's the only person in this household I can respect.

But right now, though my stomach is growling, I really want to finish this poem.

"Can I eat up here?"

Yet another frown from Mom. I wonder if I should mention the wrinkle potential of all this scowling on her delicately aging complexion.

"That is up to you," she says stiffly. "However, I think it would be nice if you decided to socialize with your family."

Socialize. Right. Is that what they're calling being lectured to these days? 'Cause I know from experience that's all that's going to happen during dinner if I attend.

Don't chew with your mouth open, Dawn. Use your napkin. Do you really need so much butter on that roll? After all, you don't want to start gaining weight.

But again, this is a battle I won't win. So I close my Algebra book and nod my head. "Fine. I'll be there in a minute," I say, purposely using my most exasperated tone.

My mother droops her shoulders, as if I'm some awful burden she has to bear on a daily basis, and exits the room. When the door closes, I pull out my half-finished poem and read it through one last time. It's really good. One of the best things I've ever written.

Somehow I have to find a chance to finish it before the deadline.

Chapter Three

Oh, this is just great.

All I wanted was fifteen minutes to finish my poem. So I skipped gym class. I mean, people skip gym class all the time. The teacher never notices. But the one time I don't show up, he pays attention. And the next thing I know, I'm being summoned to the assistant principal's office and assigned detention.

The Evil Ones are so going to kick my butt.

I trudge into Room 102, aka after-school prison, and plop down at a desk near the back. Several other far more deserving juvenile delinquents are already here. The kind of kids who have tattoos and skip class to drink beer behind the school. They stare at me with their overconfident smirks, perhaps wondering why the girl who hangs out with the cheerleaders is doomed to join their ranks this afternoon.

At least I'll have time to finish my poem, though it'll have to be published posthumously, seeing as I'll be dead by the time they put out the magazine. The Evil Ones will see to that. And no, I'm not exaggerating. You should see what they do when I get a B on my progress report. And that's nothing compared to detention.

But I can't do anything about that now. So I pull out my poem and a pen and start writing. It's a bit distracting, what with the gum snapping and whispers of the other inmates, but I somehow manage to tune out most of the noise and concentrate on my verse.

"Hey, that's pretty good!"

I look up with a start. I've been so wrapped up in my world that I hadn't realized the new girl, the supposed Satan-worshipper who drinks snake blood, has sat down at the desk beside me and is eyeing my paper.

Up close, I realize she has several piercings to go along with her already punk-rock look—a diamond stud in her nose and a silver hoop embedded in her eyebrow. Her face is pale white, almost as if she's powdered it, and her eyes, a striking blue, are rimmed with a ton of black. She really does look like Amy Lee from Evanescence. That or a gothed-out Avril Lavigne.

"You read my poem?" I ask, feeling my cheeks flush. I mean, sure, I realize that if I win the poetry contest lots of people will end up reading it, but still, her peeking over my shoulder without permission seems a grave invasion of privacy. And what if she goes and tells everyone that I, Dawn Miller, friend of the Ashleys, was seen writing poetry in detention? I might as well put in my application for the loserville lunch table right now.

Then again, she said it was good. Since I've never shown my scribblings to anyone before, I've never gotten an unbiased opinion on them. I mean, sure, I like them, but obviously I'm a bit prejudiced.

"Are you just saying that?" I ask. " 'Cause you so don't have to."

She shakes her head, causing her straight black hair to flip from side to side. "No way," she says. "I never say things I don't mean. Life's too short." She pauses, then adds, "I was assuming it'd be bad, actually. But I guess you can't judge a Barbie by its cover."

I frown. "I'm not a Barbie." I just hang out with them.

She shrugs. "Maybe you are, maybe you aren't. Honestly, I don't care either way. But you *are* a good writer."

A good writer. She thinks I'm a good writer. No one's ever told me that before. I feel a warm pride settle over me and I decide to ignore the Barbie comment. Or at least prove her wrong.

"Thanks," I say. "There's this poetry contest I want to enter it in and—"

"Oh, the one in *Faces*?"

I stare at her in shock. "How do you—?"

"I read *Faces* all the time. It's a great mag."

Wow. She actually reads literary magazines. My friends wouldn't be caught dead reading literary magazines. In fact, we have a saying: If it's not *Cosmo*, it's crap.

"I'm Dawn," I say, extending a hand.

"Starr." She shakes my hand. I notice she has on black fingernail polish that's half flaked off.

Starr. What a cool name.

"You're the headmaster's daughter, right?" I ask, assuming at least that part of the Satan-worshipping, snake-eating rumor is true.

19

"Yeah. Got kicked out of my European boarding school and so I'm stuck in this hellhole now."

Wow. I wonder what she did to get kicked out. It had to be something pretty bad, I'd think. What would it be like to be a bad girl? Not to care what people think of you? To break the rules and buck authority? I bet her parents don't dare schedule her life. And if they try, she probably laughs in their faces and then goes out and gets a new tattoo, just to spite them.

". . . and first day here, Sister Wart Nose catches me smoking in the bathroom and sentences me to detention," Starr is explaining. "I mean, for smoking! In Europe, everyone our age smokes. Massachusetts is so puritanical. It drives me absolutely insane."

I nod sympathetically, not sure how to respond. Of course I'm not a smoker, so I can't relate. But suddenly, I have the undying urge to impress her somehow. Make her see I'm more than just an airhead who happens to be able to write. Which is odd, since most people at Sacred Mary's do everything in their power to try to impress *me* and my crowd, not the other way around. But Starr doesn't seem to care that I'm one of the Populars. On the contrary, that status seems a negative in her book. Which makes her seem even cooler, somehow.

"That ring rocks," I say at last, noting the silver spider on her index finger. One thing I've learned from the Ashleys—when stuck for something to say, compliment their wardrobe. Works every time.

She smiles and waves her hand in the air, allowing the ring to catch the light and sparkle. Evidently even punk-rock chicks aren't immune to flattery. "Thanks. I got it at this really cool thrift store in Boston." She pauses for a moment, as if deciding something. Then she says, "You know, I'm planning on heading there after detention, if you want to come."

I raise my eyebrows. "You're going to Boston? How are you going to get there? Do you have a car?"

"Nah." She shakes her head. "I'm only fifteen. No license. But there's a train about a block away."

She planned to hop a train? I try to imagine what The Evil Ones would do to me if they found out I'd hopped a train to the big city. Would they kill me quickly or devise a slow, torturous death to make sure I'm really, really sorry I disobeyed?

"Come with me!" Starr says eagerly. "I know some killer used record stores."

I shake my head. "I'm already missing gymnastics 'cause of detention. My parents will totally kick my butt if I miss my Japanese tutoring as well."

Starr raises a pierced eyebrow. "Oh," she says, her tone a bit colder than before. "I understand." But she doesn't sound like she understands. In fact, she sounded more like she thinks I'm the lamest girl on the planet.

Boring Barbie, that's me.

It's so not fair. I never get to do anything fun. Run off to the big city on a whim. I suddenly envy Starr and her laissez-faire attitude on life.

Envy her and want to be her.

Maybe I could call my tutor and tell him I'm sick. And then call The Evil Ones and tell them I'm going over to one of the Ashleys' houses to work on a class project after my lesson. That should buy me at least 'til nine o'clock. Plenty of time to hit Boston and get back before they realize I'm gone.

I feel a strange thrill well up deep inside. You know what? I'm going to do it.

For once, I'm going to be a bad girl.

"Maybe I will go to Boston with you," I say, trying to keep my voice casual as my excitement takes hold. "Sounds like fun."

Chapter Four

Boston is a whole new world with Starr as my tour guide. Sure, I've been to the city before. The Evil Ones take me shopping for school clothes every autumn and to the *Nutcracker* every Christmas. But those experiences pale in comparison to Starr's Boston.

After getting sprung from detention, I drop my poem and entry form in the mail and then Starr and I head to the train station. Luckily we don't have to wait long since I've suddenly developed this huge paranoia that my dad's going to drive by and catch me. But of course he doesn't. Still, my heart's beating a mile a minute as the whistle blows and the train pulls out of the station. No turning back now.

Starr fills the half-hour trip with wild tales of boarding school (wow!), her environmental concerns (gas guzzling SUVs—bad; hybrid, environmentally friendly Toyota Prius—good), even (yay!) politics (not a big George Bush fan, to say the least).

And bonus—she never once mentions shoes, jeans, or

anything remotely related to fashion, which is soooo refreshing.

When we arrive in Boston's North Station, we take the subway to Newbury Street where we hit Urban Outfitters for funky clothes, Silver Nation for retro jewelry, and then Mystery Train, a used record store for tune'age.

In Mystery Train's low-lit basement store, Starr contents herself to flip through the seemingly endless bins of used records, pulling out and examining obscure recordings I've never even heard of. Bands with names like Joy Division and Sisters of Mercy and Bauhaus.

"This is a great album," she says, holding up a recording from a band called The Cure. "And it's not as hardcore as the others. In fact, even a Barbie like you might appreciate it."

I take the album from her, wishing she'd cut the Barbie crap. There's a pair of bright red lips on the cover and songs like "Torture," "The Snake Pit," and "A Thousand Hours" listed.

"Sounds like a barrel of laughs," I say. "Do they, um, have it on CD?"

Starr blinks. "You know, records are the authentic recordings of the music as it was meant to sound, before electronic enhancements messed with its purity."

"Sure, I get it. But I don't have a record player." I shrug. "Is it available on iTunes? I could download it. . . ."

Starr rolls her eyes. Why do I feel so incredibly unhip around her? I mean, she's the one who listens to vinyl—even the ancient Evil Ones have moved on to CDs. But her purposeful, pig-headed rejection of technology just makes her seem even cooler for some odd reason.

She yanks the record from my hands, pulling it from its dusty, cardboard sleeve and sets it on an empty turntable against the wall. Then she places the needle on the record and hands me the attached headphones.

As I put them over my ears, a dark, intense music bombards my senses. A man purrs and wails in a powerful, soul-wrenching voice. It's so deep. So beautiful. Like nothing I've ever heard before. I close my eyes to better take in the sound. It may seem completely corny, but I get the feeling this kind of music could change someone's life, if they let it.

"What do you think?" Starr asks a few minutes later, as she pulls the headphones from my ears. I reluctantly relinquish them, blinking my eyes, still a bit dazed.

"Awesome," I say, though the word seems kind of inadequate to express how the music has affected me.

"A little different from your average Beyoncé, huh?"

I frown. "Just 'cause I've never heard of this band doesn't mean I like Beyoncé, you know."

"Okay, then, what kind of music *do* you listen to?" The question has a definite challenge embedded in it and I feel my face heat as I try to figure out how to answer her. I never tell anyone what music I listen to. I'm afraid they'll just make fun of me. But Starr is different. . . .

"Let me guess," she says, regarding me with unabashed disdain. "Usher? Dave Matthews? Avril Lavigne? Linkin Park?"

"Actually, I prefer the classics," I admit at last. What the heck, it's better than having her assume I like Dave Matthews. "Rolling Stones, The Animals, Beatles, David Bowie."

"Oh! David Bowie rocks," Starr says, eyes shining and disdain quickly fleeing her face. In fact, she actually looks a bit impressed. Score one for Barbie.

"You like him?" I've never met anyone under thirty who liked David Bowie. "I've had a total crush on him since I saw *Labyrinth* when I was a kid."

"Oh, yeah, he was way sexy in that movie," Starr agrees. "I never understood why Jennifer Connelly chose saving her baby brother over him." She steps forward, in total actress mode. "Through dangers untold and hardships unnumbered, I have fought my way here to the castle beyond the Goblin City to take back the child that you have stolen."

I giggle at her rendition. "For my will is as strong as yours, and my kingdom is as great. You have no power over me," I continue, in my best dramatic voice.

"He'd have a heck of a lot of power over me wearing those tights, I'll tell you what," Starr says with a laugh. She lifts the record off the turntable and puts it back in its sleeve. "You know, Barbie, you're not half as clueless as I'd guessed."

"Gee, thanks." I roll my eyes, but I'm secretly pleased.

"I'm going to buy this for you," she says, holding up the Cure album. "And I'll even give you a break and get it on CD."

"You don't have to," I start to say, but she waves me off.

"It's all good. I like educating people about music. Music's very important."

"I agree," I say with a smile. I feel so relieved to have shared my secret music obsessions with someone who wasn't going to ridicule them because my list didn't include Eminem.

The clerk rings up her purchase and we leave the store. It's getting dark, so I suggest we catch the next train back. Don't want to get home too late and feel the wrath of The Evil Ones.

Because if I don't get caught this time, I'll be able to play bad girl again. Something I definitely want to do.

Chapter Five

"So if you were given a thousand dollars and could only pick one shoe store to spend it in, which would you choose?"

Just another Lunch Topic of the Day at the Ashley table. Sigh.

"Jimmy Choo, without a doubt," declares Ashley #2, swishing her long blond hair behind her.

"Really? I would have thought for sure you'd go with Manolos," Ashley #1 says, raising her perfectly arched eyebrows. She stabs at her salad with her fork.

"What about Steve Madden? He makes cool shoes," Ashley #3 pipes in. She's chowing down on a huge, juicy burger, as usual. I have no idea how the girl keeps her perfect size-five figure the way she eats.

"Are you kidding? I wouldn't be caught dead in cheap-o Steve Maddens."

"Yeah, but you could get like fifteen pairs for a thousand dollars instead of two pairs of Manolos." Ashley #3 explains the math slowly, so the other two can grasp it. "That's like, 'buy two, get thirteen pairs free.'"

"Wow. Thirteen free pairs of shoes . . ."

I stifle a yawn and resist the urge to bang my forehead against the table. Instead, I scan the caf, looking for Starr. I see her across the room, sitting with a couple of the computer nerds. They look like they're having a very animated conversation and I'm pretty sure it's not about shoes. I feel a stab of jealousy, but quickly squash it. After all, it's not like I invited her to come sit with me at lunch and she has every right to make other friends.

"Earth to Dawn! Come in, Dawn!"

"Oh, sorry," I say, turning back to my friends. "I'd go with Kate Spade."

The Ashleys nod knowingly. "Ooh, good choice," says Ashley #1. "Like those pink strappy sandals, right?"

"Yeah," I say halfheartedly. I wonder how'd they react if I'd said Doc Marten combat boots like Starr wears.

You know, I seriously can't believe these boring, self-absorbed people are my best friends. What's wrong with me? How did I end up here? I think about my afternoon hanging with Starr and how fun it was. How much more interesting our non-fashion related conversations were.

I got home yesterday and luckily The Evil Ones were out at a Save the Fill-in-the-Blank charity event so I didn't have to explain my absence or my detention. Magda heated me up a plate of yummy enchiladas with extra spice, which I took up to my room. There, I uploaded the new Cure CD onto my iPod and listened to it while doing homework. It's probably the best CD I've heard in my entire life. I fell asleep with my headphones on and had the coolest dreams.

Now I'm back to reality. Mundane, shallow reality. I

wonder what the Ashleys would do if I got up from the lunch table and walked over to sit with Starr. Would they simply tease me or disown me forever?

Sadly, I'm not ready to find out. I mean, I barely know Starr. And I'm not even sure she likes me. Sure, she tolerates me, but she calls me Barbie, for goodness sake. Like I'm some doll she's playing with. And I'm not about to risk losing my only friends, plastic though they may be, just on this crazy notion of me becoming a bad girl.

I'd rather straddle the fence a while longer and see which side I end up falling on.

"That CD is fab!" I catch up to Starr as she's walking out of school. I notice she's changed from her uniform into a long-sleeved, black-netted top. On her lower half, she's completed the outfit with a black skirt, fishnets, and combat boots. Silver rings adorn almost every finger and she has a stack of rubber bracelets up her left arm.

She turns around and smiles indulgently, as if addressing a small child. "Glad you like it," she says. I wonder if she's ticked at me for not finding her at lunch. For not inviting her to the Ashley table. But then I figure she's probably not interested in hanging around with them anyhow. I mean, I can hardly tolerate them myself and they're supposedly my best friends.

"So, where you headed?" I ask.

"I was thinking of going downtown, actually. I heard there's a bunch of skaters who hang out under this parking deck and do tricks. I want to go check them out."

"Skaters?"

"Yeah, you know, skateboarders, Barbie. Those guys

with big, baggy pants who ride around on wooden boards with wheels?"

"I know what skateboarders are," I say, exasperated. She really does think I'm a moron. "That sounds, uh, cool."

"Yeah, should be," Starr says. Then pauses. It's an awkward pause and I realize she's not going to invite me this time. Maybe she filled her Barbie quota for the month yesterday and wishes I'd just leave her alone.

I'm supposed to be at a yearbook committee meeting in five minutes, anyhow. And if I don't show up to year-book, the other committee members might accidentally put the wrong cheerleader on page forty-three, which of course would be a complete disaster.

Yes, my life is that lame.

"Well, I'll catch you around, then," I say, knowing I sound disappointed and pathetic. When did I turn into such a loser? Hanging around and waiting for an invita-tion? That's so not me. At least it never used to be.

"Wanna come with?" Starr asks at last.

Woot! "Um, well, yeah, I guess," I say, keeping my voice uber-casual. Like it's no big deal either way. "Sure."

"Okay. Let's go catch the bus then."

Since two out of three Ashleys already have their licenses and matching BMWs, this public transportation thing is a new concept to me. In fact, before now, I hadn't even known our town had a bus line. But sure enough, minutes later, a big gray vehicle pulls up to the bench we've been waiting on and opens its doors. We pay our dollar and scamper to the back.

Starr pulls out a pair of headphones and places them

over her ears, effectively preventing any chatting on the way there. But I'm cool with it. Instead, I stare out the window and watch the world I know—subdivisions, shopping malls, and upscale restaurants—slowly morph into a much more depressing scene.

The mansions with their perfect paint jobs and meticulously landscaped yards melt into rickety triple-decker apartment buildings with sagging porches and trash-filled yards. The shopping malls with their Macy's and Filene's anchor stores are replaced by small, squat, stand-alone shops advertising Bail Bonds, Pawn Shops, and Cash Advances. And the restaurants with their surf and turf specials have downsized into $4.99 all-you-can-eat buffets, and an obscene number of McDonald's squat on nearly every corner.

I'd never been to this side of town and if The Evil Ones knew I was here now, they'd be freaked out beyond belief. Probably worry that some pimp would force drugs down my throat and I'd be a crackhead hooker by morning. But for some reason their imagined disapproval makes the whole experience even more thrilling.

Right now, no one knows where I am. I can do whatever I want and no one will see me. Judge me. Tell me what to do. I know it sounds completely melodramatic, but I feel free for the first time in my life.

The bus pulls up to a street corner and Starr jumps up from her seat. I follow her out of the bus in nervous anticipation. We're now leaving the security of a moving vehicle and heading out into unfamiliar territory. I tuck my Coach purse a little tighter under my arm, just in case.

"They supposedly hang out under this parking deck

down here," Starr says, pointing the way. "Until the cops come and kick them out, of course."

Of course. The cops. "They won't, um, arrest anyone, will they?" I ask, a bit worried. I'm so not ready to make that one phone call to The Evil Ones to tell them I've been brought downtown for cavorting with juvenile delinquents.

Starr snorts. "Relax, Barbie," she says, and I feel my face heat again. Why did I even ask that? I'm so uncool, it's not even funny.

We walk down the hill, sticking to the crumbling sidewalk, until we come to a two-story, concrete parking structure. As we step underneath its top floor, loud banging sounds echo throughout—like thunder claps warning of an approaching storm.

The skaters.

We follow the noise until we come to a group of about six guys, all dressed similarly in baggy shorts, colored sneakers and shirts with logos like "Independent" and "Alien Workshop" scrawled across them. Most have wild, colorful tattoos inked onto their legs and arms.

"Hey, guys," Starr says as she picks a curb to squat down on. Several skaters nod and wave before continuing their tricks, as if they're used to girls coming down to watch. And they probably are. I'm sure skaters get a lot of groupies.

I sit down next to Starr, trying not to think about what the grimy sidewalk will do to my school uniform and whether I have a clean one hanging in my closet. I should have changed like she had. Not just for the dirt factor, but also the geekazoid factor.

"Dude, ollie up on that curb and grind it," one of the skaters shouts to his friend. I watch as the friend steps onto his board with one foot, kicks up some speed, then bends his knees to jump onto the curb. He slides for a bit, the base of his board running against the curb, then pops off with a flourish.

But it's not the trick itself that impresses me. It's the boy who performs it who has captured my attention. I can't believe what a total hottie he is. Unlike some of the more punked-out-looking skaters, he has short, somewhat curly blond hair and a sweet, boyish face. Chad Michael Murray with grungy skater clothes. Majorly yummy and so much cooler than the meatheads and preps we get at Sacred Mary's.

"He's way cute," I say, nudging Starr. She gives me one of those I Barely Tolerate Your Patheticness stares.

"Yeah, he's all right," she says, not really sounding like she thinks so. "But look at him." She points to a scruffy-looking guy with a black mohawk, his arms completely sleeved in tattoos. A guy I wouldn't want to meet in a dark alley and certainly not one I'd want to date. But hey, different strokes for different folks. At least I wouldn't have any competition for "Chad."

"Yeah, he's cool," I say absently, turning my gaze back to my new crush. He picks that moment, of course, to turn around as well, and he totally catches me staring at him! OMG—how embarrassing!

I quickly look down, studying the ground as if I've lost an earring or something. After a few moments, I peek to see if it's safe to look up again. He's still watching me from across the way, a faint smile playing at the corners of his lips. But not an overconfident I Am Better Than You smile like the ones Starr indulges me with when she thinks I'm being naive and Barbie-like. Rather a curious, nice smile. Almost as if he's interested in coming to talk to me.

I hope he does.

Starr snorts. "I think he likes you, Barbie."

My heart leaps at her words and I can feel my pulse kick up a few notches in anticipation. "You do?" I ask. "Should I go talk to him?"

"Nah, wait for him to come talk to you," she suggests. "You don't want to appear too eager."

True. I don't. And I'm not, either. As cute as he is, it's not like I'm going to try to hook up with him or anything. I mean, he's a skater from the so-called wrong side of town. The Evil Ones would never, ever let me date him and the whole thing would end up so *Romeo and Juliet* tragic.

The mohawked skater flips up his board with his foot and catches the other end with his left hand. Then he walks over to where we're sitting and squats down to face us.

"Nice piercing," he says to Starr, motioning to her eyebrow.

"Thanks," she says coolly, as if she gets complimented on it all the time and it's no big deal.

"I just did my tongue."

I widen my eyes in interest as Mohawk sticks out his tongue, revealing a silver stud imbedded in its center.

"Wow, did that hurt?" I ask before I can stop myself.

Starr and Mohawk both simultaneously give me a look,

as if to say, "A/B Conversation, Barbie. Why don't you 'C' your way out of it?"

"Cool. I've been dying to get my tongue pierced," Starr says, turning back to Mohawk.

"There's a place down the street that does it. Wanna do it now?"

"Sure." Starr shrugs. As if he's asked her to get a soda and not jam a silver spike through her own flesh. She scrambles up from her sitting position. "Let's go."

"What about her?" Mohawk asks, nodding at me.

"Wanna get pierced, Barbie?" Starr asks, her voice laced with sarcasm.

"Um," I flounder. I want to go with them, but it's already approaching five o'clock. If I miss another session of Japanese tutoring, the guy's bound to tell on me and then The Evil Ones will start asking questions,

"Where you guys going?" The Chad skater interrupts, effectively making my heart skip a beat. I hadn't heard him approach.

"Todd's Tattoos," says Mohawk. "Tongue piercing."

"Cool. I wanna come." He kicks up his skateboard, grabs his Von Dutch hat from the curb, and heads toward us.

"Okay, I guess I'll come, too," I say, my stomach churning with spooked butterflies. I mean, how can one seriously pass up a chance to be up close and personal with the skater hottie? Sure, I'm risking The Evil Ones' wrath, but I should be okay; how long can piercing take? Starr gives a little sniff, as if to say, "You're so obvious," but I just laugh.

We head down the trash-lined street, Starr and

Mohawk leading the way, talking animatedly about tattoos and other forms of body torture. Chad falls in step with me, much to my delight.

"I'm Sean, by the way," he says, glancing over at me with a shy smile.

"Hi, Sean. I'm Dawn," I say, then can't help a giggle as I realize our names rhyme. If we got married, everyone would always tease us about it at dinner parties. "Sean and Dawn," they'd say. "How nauseatingly cute." And we'd lovingly smile at one another and then back at our guests. "Guess it was meant to be," we'd say.

Not that I'm picking out china patterns quite yet, mind you. After all, I've known the guy for all of about five seconds. I don't even know if he thinks I'm cute or not.

"I've never seen you around here," Sean is saying. "Do you go to Woodbury High? I'm a senior there."

Ooh, a senior. An older man!

I shake my head. "I go to Sacred Mary's."

A pause, then, "Oh."

I cringe. It's hard to believe a single one-syllable word can contain so much condemnation.

"Not 'cause I want to, obviously," I quickly add. "The Evil Ones don't give me as much as a multiple-choice questionnaire when scheduling my life."

He raises an eyebrow. "Evil Ones?"

I smile sheepishly. "Yeah, like, aka Mom and Dad."

"Ah," he says, grinning, condemnation gone. "The Evil Ones. I like that. I've got an Evil One at home myself."

I can feel my cheeks heat again and I resist the urge to do the flippy thing with my hair that all girls do when they're talking to boys. I'm so glad I decided to wear it loose today and not bound up in braids as usual. Way too Swiss Miss for the downtown crowd.

I sneak a peek at him out of the corner of my eye. God, he's cute. Up close, now I can see he has the most sparkling blue eyes. And ears that stick out a little, in the most adorable way. He's probably about 5'11", slender and muscular—must be from the skateboarding. And his smile is sweet. Genuine.

In short, major yumage.

We reach the back alley shack called Todd's Tattoos and go inside. The grisly, heavyset guy (Todd?) behind the counter seems to know Mohawk and addresses him as "Eddie."

"Come on, Eddie," he says with a chuckle. "You got nothing left to pierce, do you?"

Mohawk, err . . . Eddie laughs. "Nah, not me today, Todd. Starr here wants her tongue pierced."

The man nods approvingly and motions for Starr to sit down in a red vinyl swingy chair. Then he rummages behind the counter for the appropriate piercing gear. I wonder how sterile his needles are.

Starr flashes me an excited smile and I smile back. Then, when Sean turns his back to examine the walls of tattoo designs, she nods toward him, then gives me a thumbs-up. I stifle a pleased giggle.

Todd walks over to Starr and rips open a paper package containing the hugest needle known to mankind. I stare in shock. They're going to put *that* through her tongue? I want to ask her if she's sure she wants to do this, but don't want to sound like a Barbie again.

Starr promptly sticks out her tongue, looking as if she

doesn't have a fear in the world. I wish I had her confidence. Or tolerance for pain, at least. The man rubs numbing solution on her tongue, then readies the needle. At the last minute I turn away, not able to watch the sharp object penetrate her.

When I turn back a moment later, it's over. There's now a silver stud embedded in Starr's tongue. Eddie gives her an atta-girl woot and she smiles.

"Did it hurt?" I ask.

She shakes her head. "Nawh that mucthh."

"It may be hard to talk for a day or two," Eddie informs her. "But trust me, it's worth it."

"Anyone else?" Todd the torturer asks.

"Dawhhn," says Starr, pointing at me.

"What? No way," I protest. "I am so not having my tongue pierced."

"Bahhbie."

"I'm not a Barbie. Just 'cause I don't want a big metal spike jammed through my mouth does not make me a Barbie."

"Hey, babe, chill," Eddie says. "Give the girl a break. Even you gotta admit, a tongue's pretty hardcore for a first piercing."

Yeah, I say, mentally thanking Eddie for his voice of reason.

"How about your navel?" Todd suggests.

"Navel?"

"Yeah, you know. Belly button," says Eddie, gesturing to my middle.

"I don't know . . ." I wonder how many coolness

points I'll lose if I run screaming from the piercing parlor. Probably all, since I don't have that many to begin with.

But still, I can't get anything pierced. Not even my belly button. The Evil Ones would kill me . . .

. . . *if* they found out, that is. And there's no way they could—if I play my cards right. It's not like they ever see me naked, so unless I wore a half-shirt or bikini in front of them, they'd probably never know. . . .

"Forhget ith, Eddie," says swollen-tongued Starr. She rises from the piercing chair. "She'th too scared."

"I'm not scared," I retort, sick of Starr's jabs. I plop down on the chair and pull my shirttail out of my skirt. "Go ahead. Pierce away."

Starr, Eddie, and Sean look impressed by my random act of defiance. The tattoo guy chuckles, as if he's seen these kinds of dares a million times. He goes back behind the counter to get a clean needle.

Starr and Eddie, mission accomplished, wander off to go look at some silver and leather jewelry. Sean approaches and kneels down beside me, his intense blue eyes searching my face.

"Are you sure you want to do this?" he asks.

"Yes," I say firmly, even though I'm totally not.

"Don't let them goad you into something you don't want," he says earnestly. "You've got nothing to prove."

I appreciate him saying that, but I realize that in this case, he's wrong. I do have something to prove. To myself. This piercing will be more than just a hole in my abdomen and a new piece of jewelry. It's a symbol of me taking control of my life. Of doing things the way I want to do them, even if those things don't fit into The Evil Ones' plan. Even if they are looked down upon by my air-head friends. By piercing my belly button, I'm saying that I'm my own person. And I'll do things my way.

"I'm sure," I say.

The man returns with his needle. It's even bigger than the tongue one and for a moment I feel like I'm going to pass out. He paints a black dot on my stomach with a marker and then places a clamp in the fold of skin.

At that point, the point when I'm ready to completely wimp out and beg for mercy, Sean grabs hold of my trembling hand. I look over at him and he smiles at me. A pure, beautiful, genuine smile of support and encouragement.

"Just look at me," he says. "It'll be easier that way."

The pain is hot. The needle burns through my skin and I bite down not to scream in agony. It's quite possibly the worst pain I've ever felt in my entire life—including the time I broke my arm in third grade. I squeeze Sean's hand tightly, my nails digging into his palm and I try to concentrate on looking into his eyes. Losing myself in their beautiful blue.

And then it's over. I survive. And I have a cool new piece of silver jewelry embedded in my body.

"Whoo hoo!" I cry, jumping up. "I did it!" Unable to stop myself, I throw my arms around Sean in celebration. He laughs and hugs me back, carefully, so as not to bump the piercing.

"No sex for twenty-four hours," Todd instructs, causing both of us to pull away from our embrace and blush deep red.

"We're . . . not . . . I mean, um," I stammer. Ah, hell.

Todd nods knowingly and I get the feeling he's thinking the lady doth protest too much. But "That'll be twenty bucks," is all he says.

I pay him and the four of us walk out of the shop. We hit the diner next door and order burgers, fries and Cokes. (Starr orders a yogurt smoothie to numb her tongue.) We chat and joke and laugh during the meal. Starr and Eddie get into a big debate about the war in Iraq at one point. While they banter and bicker, Sean and I poke fun at them from across the table.

We're having such a blast, I lose track of time. For a few blissful minutes, I totally forget about my commitments. About The Evil Ones and the torture they will have planned for me if I get home late with no good explanation as to where I have been.

We walk out of the restaurant and I realize it's now nearly six o'clock and I *have* to get back home. Starr grudgingly agrees to go with me, after she says her good-byes to Eddie. I'm a bit disturbed to realize her good-byes include jamming her tongue down his throat at the bus stop. After all, she just met the guy! Not to mention that said tongue was recently traumatized by a large needle. But I guess that's what you do when you're a bad girl.

I laugh a little, embarrassed, and turn from the major PDA-age. Sean rolls his eyes and takes me by the shoulder, leading me a few yards away.

"Looks like Eddie finally met his match," he says with a chuckle.

"He's not a jerk, is he?" I ask. I don't know why I feel the need to worry about Starr. Of all people, she doesn't

Mari Mancusi

need a protector, that's for sure. Especially not someone like me. But I can't help being a mother hen.

Sean shakes his head. "Nah, he's cool. Just loud." He smiles. "That's nice of you, though. To look out for your friend."

I shrug. "She's not even really my friend. In fact, I'm not even sure she likes me much."

"No?" Sean asks, reaching over to brush a lock of hair out of my eyes. "Why wouldn't she like you?"

His sudden close proximity starts doing funny things to my pulse. Does he want to kiss me? I swallow hard and drop my gaze to the dirty sidewalk. I'm such a wimp.

He puts a finger under my chin and tilts my head up so I'm looking into his eyes. OMG, this is it. He is going to kiss me! I'm going to be kissed by the gorgeous Sean. I can feel his warm, peppermint breath on my face.

"Well, I like you," he says with a grin. "I mean, just FYI."

"Do you?" I ask, regretting the words the second they leave my mouth. What a dork. I should have said, "I like you, too."

"Dawn, the bus ith here," Starr calls. "Hurry upth!"

Sean releases my chin and steps back. He looks a bit dazed. Then he laughs it off.

"Can I get your digits?" he asks.

I nod, pulling a marker from my purse. Feeling brave and saucy all of a sudden, I take his hand and scribble my cell number across his palm. Then I smile, toss my hair, and run to catch the bus. I don't look back.

I make my way to the rear of the bus, where Starr is waiting for me.

"Ooh, lovahh girl," she teases.

"Speak for yourself," I retort. "I'm not the one with my tongue down a boy's throat an hour after getting it pierced."

Starr laughs and sticks out her pierced tongue at me. "It already feels better," she says. "How's the belly button?"

"Still sore." I yank down my skirt so the wool doesn't rub against the sensitive skin.

"Regret it?"

"No way. It was great." And it was. There was some kind of power in it. Hard to explain, but it was there. Like I'd broken the chains of good-girlism and would never be the same. "I'd do it again in a heartbeat."

I look over to catch Starr studying me, a thoughtful look on her face. "You know, Barbie," she says. "You may be okay after all."

"Gee, thanks," I say sarcastically.

But deep inside, I'm dancing.

Chapter Six

"Dawn, where have you been?"

I drop my book bag on the hallway floor and drag my feet into the living room where The Evil Ones are glaring at me, expecting me to provide some kind of reasonable explanation for my absence. Evidently the Japanese tutor called and ratted me out.

But I'm prepared. "Yearbook ran late," I say. I worked out the perfect excuse on the bus ride back to the proverbial "right side of town." "We were having so much fun picking out photos we completely lost track of time. Tell Hoshiko I'm sorry."

Dad furrows his bushy eyebrows at me, as if trying to tunnel into my brain and determine whether I'm lying. Honestly, I get the feeling he can do this sometimes. But in this case, evidently my mental shield is too tough to penetrate 'cause all he says is, "You need to call if you're not going to make your tutoring. Those classes cost money, you know."

As if he's worried about money. Thanks to my grandparents, we have enough to last two lifetimes. I could miss Japanese lessons from now until next Christmas and it wouldn't put so much as a dent in his bank account.

"Yes, Dad," I say. "I'm sorry."

"We got a note from your gym teacher today, Dawn," my mother breaks in. "How come you didn't tell us you got detention?"

Oh, great. I'd nearly forgotten about that.

"You were out last night at the Save the Whatever party," I say. "I was going to tell you tonight."

"Detention!" My dad rages from his chair. He wags a finger at me. "Do you think Harvard accepts students who get detentions?"

I'm not sure about that one, but if the answer turns out to be, "No, they turn them down flat," I might have to score a few more this year, just to ensure I'm completely blacklisted from the Ivy League nightmare.

"Jeez, Dad, it's not like I'm some juvenile delinquent or something," I protest. I've worked this one out, too. "It's simple. I had major crampage so I skipped gym."

This makes my dad's face go all red, as I knew it would. He doesn't like to think about his fifteen-year-old daughter's monthly feminine functions.

"Well, don't let it happen again," he grunts, turning back to his book. Heh. I should play the period card more often.

"Don't worry," I say, grabbing my book bag from the floor. "I'm going up to do my homework now."

I dash up the stairs and into my room before they can bring up any of my other shortcomings. After all, it's not often I win a battle with them and I'm so going to take all the victory I can get.

Bad Girl Dawn, one. Evil Ones, zero.

I lie back on my bed and lift my shirt a few inches, rotating the belly-button ring as Todd had instructed me to do. It looks so cool and I'm way proud of myself for going through with it. The old wimpy Dawn would never have been able to bear all that pain. And I'm willing to bet none of the Ashleys would have, either.

I've got a big test tomorrow and I know I should start studying, but all I want to do is close my eyes and think about the dreamy Sean. I pull my knees up to my chest, hugging them close, feeling that warm squishy feeling you get when you first meet someone yummy.

You know, I think if that bus hadn't come right then, he would have kissed me. I wonder what it'd be like. I'm a bit ashamed to say I've only kissed three guys in my entire fifteen years on the planet and one of those doesn't count 'cause it was during Spin the Bottle. I wonder if Sean kisses more with his lips—like you see people do in the movies—or with his tongue—like you see everyone doing in the school hallways.

Well, one thing's for sure. I'm bound and determined to find out, firsthand.

I can't believe I slept ten hours last night. I thought I'd just close my eyes for five seconds and then start studying for my test. Instead I fell asleep and only woke up when my alarm started blaring at five A.M.

To make matters worse, it's raining, so crew practice on the river totally sucked. Now I'm in school and completely unprepared for my Chemistry test. The Evil Ones are going to kill me if I flunk.

But for some reason, that doesn't make me feel as creeped out as it normally would. Not when I still have the Sean warm-fuzzies tickling my insides. I wonder when he'll call me.

I'm in English class when my cell phone starts vibrating. As the teacher turns to write something on the blackboard, I surreptitiously pull it out of my bag. There's a text message.

>*How R U?*

Hmm. Don't recognize the number it's from. I glance up to make sure the teacher is still distracted and then text back.

>*K. Who r u?*

>*Sean.* ☺

OMG—it's Sean! Sean is texting me! How cool is that? My fingers are literally trembling as I type in my reply.

>*Hi!! U in skool?*

>*Ya. Bored.*

Luckily, I rock at texting. I can do it underneath my desk without the teacher catching me. Though she's so wrapped up in the saga of Hamlet and how he can't seem to make the simple decision of whether "to be or not to be," she probably wouldn't notice if I had a full-on voice convo at the back of the classroom.

>*What r u doing after skool?*

After school? Is he just making conversation or asking me out on a date? It is Friday, after all. And if he is asking me out, should I tell him the truth? That I have gymnastics and then tutoring and then homework? That I can't possibly skip out on my life for a third day in a row without getting grounded for a millennium? Even though it is a weekend night?

Nah.

>*Nuthin. U?*

>*Sk8ing.*

Oh. I slump in my chair. Guess he wasn't asking me out after all. Now he probably thinks I'm a loser with no life. I'm not sure what to text back, but before I can decide, another message pops up.

>*Later E & I going 2 a rave. U & S want 2 com?*

A rave? He wants us to go to a rave? Like one of those all-night, techno dance parties held in warehouses? I try to imagine myself announcing to The Evil Ones that I'm going to a rave and won't be home 'til morning.

Can you say "No effing way?"

>*Can't. Sorry* ☹ *Will ask S tho.*

I reluctantly hit send and beam the disappointing message to Sean's cell phone. This sucks. I've probably totally blown my chances with him now. He's going to think I'm some goodie-two-shoes type. But what else can I do? There's absolutely no way I can go to a rave, as much as I'd like to.

Did I mention how much my life blows?

Chapter Seven

"If you could buy only one kind of makeup—I'm talking lip gloss, eyeliner and mascara even—where would you buy it?"

Ashley #2: "Stila counter, definitely."

Ashley #1: "Really? I would have said Hard Candy. They have the coolest shades and the best glitter eye pencils known to mankind."

Ashley #3: "I just really like Cover Girl."

Pause. Turn to stare in sync.

"I wouldn't be caught dead wearing Cover—hey, Dawn, where are you going?"

I've had enough. I can literally feel brain cells dying as I sit next to these self-absorbed makeup morons. I sense their burning stares as I leave the table without a word and head down to the other half of the school lunchroom. The half I thought I'd never be forced to sit in, never mind make the conscious choice to do so. I know for a fact, I've just sealed my high-school fate. Fallen off the wrong side of the fence that I've been straddling, but for some reason, I don't care much.

"Hey, Starr," I greet as I approach her lunch table. Her fellow tablemates glare at me, perhaps wondering if I'm here on some nefarious scheme like the popular kids always seem to be hatching in the movies. Befriend the loser kid, trick her into going to the dance with the popular boy so you can pour pig's blood on her or whatever. Like the real-life popular kids are really all that creative or bored.

Starr looks up, raising a pierced eyebrow. "What's wrong, Barbie?" she asks coolly.

"Do you mind if I sit with you?" I ask, praying she'll say yes. I suddenly realize I've just walked away from my high-school social standing with no concrete idea of where I belong. If Starr's crowd rejects me, where do I go next?

Starr seems to ponder my question a moment, then moves her canvas book bag off the stool. "Free lunchroom," she says with a shrug.

Not exactly a welcoming invitation, though not a rejection either. I understand her and her tablemates' lack of enthusiasm. They know for a fact that if the situation were reversed, if Starr wanted the empty seat at my regular lunch table, there's no way the Ashleys would let her sit down, no matter how much I begged.

Bleh. High-school politics sure are interesting—in a pathetic, demeaning, scar-you-for-life kind of way.

I decide to play it friendly. "Thanks," I say in a grateful voice. "I just couldn't stand one more fashion convo."

Starr and several other tablemates break out into giggles.

"What?" I demand, a little annoyed. Are they making fun of me?

"Sorry," Starr says, regaining control of herself. "But before you came we were actually talking about who makes the best combat boots."

"Were you?" I shake my head in amusement. "Whoops." And here I thought they'd be debating the president's justification of the Iraq war or the continuing relief effort for the tsunami victims in Asia.

"What did you expect us to be talking about?" demands a boy from across the table. He's cute, if a bit on the nerdy side, with black-rimmed glasses and sandy brown hair. Sort of Clark Kentish. "Dungeons and Dragons?"

"Stuart, be nice," Starr reprimands. For a new girl, she certainly seems to have the crowd under her thumb. "Dawn's trying. But you can't completely break free of Barbiedom in one afternoon. She's made an important first step, though. And we should support her."

The boy snorts, but doesn't follow up. Instead he pulls out a Nintendo DS and starts battling space aliens or whatever you do on those things.

"That's Stuart," Starr says. "Obsessed with all things medieval and all things video-game related."

"And all-around pain in the butt," groans the girl to his right. She's really pretty, with brown curly hair and bright green eyes. She reaches out her hand. "I'm Sophie Sawyer."

"Sophie is an amazing computer genius," Starr says. "She can, like, hack websites and everything."

"Shhh," Sophie says, putting a hand to her lips. But I can tell she's pleased by Starr's description. "You're gonna make her think I'm some kind of nerd or something," she admonishes.

But I don't think that. That's the funny thing. In fact, to me, these people all seem a hundred percent cooler than any of my so-called popular friends.

"Dawn, are you, like, okay?"

Speak of the devils. I look up to see that all three Ashleys have paraded over to the table and are staring down at me, arms folded across their chests, overly concerned expressions on their faces.

"Yeah, did you, like, hit your head or something?" Ashley #2 chimes in. She's so clever.

"No, I'm fine," I say, biting my lower lip. I knew they'd be ticked at me for walking away mid-makeup convo, but I had no idea they'd actually come after me, intervention style. This is going to be a lot harder than I thought.

"Then what are you doing here? Sitting with these . . . skanky losers?" asks Ashley #1, tossing back her long blond hair.

I cringe. What do I do now? Do I laugh it off, get up and rejoin my friends? Not rock the boat of my precarious high-school existence? If I diss them now, I know for a fact, that'll be it. I'll be a reject for the next two years of high school. Blacklisted from prom committee. Not invited to any of the cool parties. Looked down upon, made fun of. Do I really want to subject myself to all of that? All because of what? I don't like to chat about shoes?

"No, you have it wrong," Starr interjects. "Dawn *was* sitting with skanky losers. She moved seats and now she's sitting with intelligent, interesting people."

"Shut up, freak. We're talking to Dawn."

I draw in a deep breath. I feel like time has frozen in place as practically everyone in the caf seems to stop eating and await my response.

Do I get up and pretend it was all a joke? Rejoin the friends I've had since kindergarten? Or do I stay put and defend the high-school helpless? The innocent people who the Ashleys trample on each and every day?

I steal a glance at Starr, who is staring at me with raised eyebrows. I realize she thinks I'm going to sell her down the river. That I'm still a Barbie underneath my brave new exterior. That I don't have the courage to stand up for my convictions or my new friends.

She's wrong.

"Uh," I stammer. "I think, um, I'm going to hang here for a bit?"

(Okay, a totally lame and not at all empowering-the-downtrodden speech, but it's the best I can come up with on such short notice.)

"Whatever, Dawn," Ashley #2 snorts. "God, when did you turn out to be such a social reject?"

And with that very snappy, clever comeback, the three Ashleys turn heel and strut back to the "cool" half of the lunchroom. It's like one of those stereotypical scenes you see in teen movies where the populars stride down the hallway in a slow-motion row, pushing away the peons who inadvertently stand in their path. It'd almost be funny if I weren't so freaked out about what I just did.

I can't believe I just told off a) the most popular girls in school, and b) my best friends. A nagging guilt immediately starts poking at my insides. It's not like the Ashleys haven't been good friends to me. I mean, sure, they're shallow and silly, but they always treated me with respect. Included me in everything . . .

I shake my head. No. They deserve this and more. Okay, they've been cool to me, but they're not cool to my new friends. Or the other three-quarters of the school lunchroom. They think they're better than everyone else and they need to be taken down a peg or two. And I'm the only person who can do it effectively. Maybe I'll end up being a high-school crusader for nerds.

I turn back to my lunch tablemates. "Sorry about that," I say, forcing my voice to stay calm. "Some people have no manners."

Stuart lets out a whoop and the whole table combusts in excited conversation. It's score one for the loser table and I'm their new champion. They excitedly recount the pissed-off looks on the Ashleys' faces.

Starr elbows me and I turn to look at her. She smiles and pats me on the shoulder.

"You know, Barbie doesn't really fit you, namewise," she says. "In fact, I'd better start calling you Dawn."

Chapter Eight

"So listen," I say after lunch, as Starr and I head to our next class. "Sean texted me this morning."

Starr grins and pokes me in my side with a black-painted fingernail. "Ooh, lover girl," she says. "I told you he likes you!"

"Yeah, yeah." I know I'm completely blushing. Who wouldn't be? "But anyway, he says there's a rave tonight and him and Eddie are going and—"

"Really?" Starr squeals. Literally squeals. "I love raves. Have you ever been to one? I went to a ton in Europe. They're so fun!" She grabs my hand. "We have to go."

I smile at her enthusiasm. "Yeah, I'm sure it'd be a blast. I can't go though, so I thought if you wanted to, you should call Eddie and—"

"No. You're going. Definitely. This'll be a great place to hook up with Sean. Why can't you go?"

"Are you kidding? The Evil Ones would never let me attend some all-night dance party. And I have a billion commitments on Saturday that I can't be tired for. I volunteer at a nursing home in the morning. Then I have—"

59

"Dawn. Darling. Let's get those priorities straightened out," Starr reprimands. "You want Sean. Sean wants you to attend the rave. End of story."

I shake my head. "You don't get it. My parents won't let me go. That's the period, end of story, we're talking about here."

"What if they didn't know?"

"Huh?"

"You can tell them you're sleeping over at my house," Starr suggests. "My dad's the headmaster. Surely they trust him to guard your virtue for the evening. I can even have him call your parents and talk to them."

"And he won't mind us going to the rave?"

"My bedroom's in the basement and I have my own exit. We can come and go as we please and he'll never know. He's a super-heavy sleeper."

A thrill of excitement bubbles in my belly as I consider her plan. It's so crazy it just might work. And I'll get to see Sean. Better yet, I'll get to dance with Sean. All night. How can I pass up this opportunity?

"Okay," I say, making my decision. "I'll call them and let them know I'm spending the night with you."

"Goodnight, girls."

"Goodnight, Dad," Starr says sweetly as her father closes her bedroom door. She waits a beat, for his footsteps to fade away, then jumps up and locks it tight.

"That takes care of him," she says with a grin.

Those pesky butterflies are country line dancing in my stomach again. I can't believe I'm here. I can't believe what we're about to do.

The Evil Ones were surprisingly receptive to my sleeping over at Starr's house. Of course when I asked, I used her given name (Ashleigh, if you can believe it!) and casually threw in the fact that her father is headmaster of our school. My Dad went as far as suggesting I sweet-talk the guy into a Harvard recommendation letter. He always has an agenda.

Starr's home is small, but cozy, in a middle-class subdivision on the east side of town. The house is a split-level, with her bedroom taking up the entire refinished basement. It's a pretty cool room, with a futon bed, beanbag chairs, a TV with DVD and PlayStation 2, and scads of musician cutouts and posters covering almost every inch of wall space. She even has a black light, which allows for some cool glow-in-the-darkage from the star stickers she pasted to her ceiling.

"So do you just live here with your dad?" I ask, after we've changed into cozy flannel Gap pajamas.

"Yeah," Starr says, flopping on her bed and grabbing the remote control.

"Where does your mother live?" I wonder what it'd be like to have divorced parents. Mine are like the only ones on the planet who are still married. Such weirdos.

Starr drops the remote control without flipping on the TV and rolls over onto her back, staring at her starred ceiling. "Nowhere," she says after a long pause. "She's dead."

Oh, nice one, Dawn. Open mouth and insert foot.

"I'm sorry," I say, joining her on the bed. "I didn't mean to—"

"It's okay," Starr assures me. "She had breast cancer. Died a year ago next week."

I look over and catch her swiping at the corner of her eyes with her sleeve. Is she crying? It's weird to see this tough, punk-rock chick looking so vulnerable.

"Sorry," she says with a choking laugh. "I never cry. It's just . . . well, I miss her sometimes, you know? And it, like, just hits me."

I don't know. I have no idea what it would be like to lose a parent. A mother. As much as I can't stand mine half the time, I do love her and couldn't imagine her not being there every night when I came home from school.

"I'm sorry, Starr," I say, reaching over to grab the box of tissues on her night table. I hand her one and she dabs her eyes. "I can't imagine how hard that must be."

I wonder if that's why Starr dresses the way she does. Acts all tough. Gets kicked out of boarding school. I wonder if she was completely different before her mother's illness and death.

"It's okay, thanks," Starr says, sitting up in bed. "I'm fine. But let's change the subject, okay?"

I nod, but am suddenly unable to think of a single other topic. Some friend I am.

Starr groans. "Okay, fine. I'll pick then. New topic of the night is boys."

"Any particular boys?" I ask, making an innocent face.

She taps her chin with her forefinger, as if pretending to think. "What about . . . Eddie and Sean?" she says with a grin.

So we talk about the skaters and way overanalyze everything they've said or done and how much fun we're going to have with them tonight and what we should do if they want to dance with us, kiss us, etc. Soon we're giggling like crazy.

After a bit, Starr turns on her PlayStation and we occupy ourselves with video games. I completely suck at them. Since video games are considered "uncool" with the Ashley crowd, I've hardly ever played. But even though my character dies on a regular basis, I still have a blast playing. Maybe I'm destined to be a nerd. . . .

At nine o'clock, Starr suggests we start getting ready. She heads to her closet to find us outfits. No way am I going to a rave in my Barbie school uniform, she says.

Now dressed in a pink baby-doll T-shirt (that nicely shows off my new piercing), low-rise baggy jeans, and colored sneakers, I feel like a new person. A cool individual, not an Ashley clone. In fact, I'm so psyched about my new look, I keep peeking in the mirror to make sure it's really me.

Starr chooses a more gothed-out outfit of black on black, of course, but she could look cool in anything.

Next it's makeup time. Starr slathers the stuff on her face while I content myself with a dab of lip gloss and a swipe of mascara. Then, feeling brave, I add a little eyeliner. Not so much as to make me look like Avril Lavigne, mind you, but enough that you'd actually notice I'm wearing makeup. It looks pretty cool, if I do say so myself.

Makeup application completed, Starr pulls me in front of her full-length mirror and we check each other out.

"We look fab, darling," she pronounces in an over-the-top English accent. "Let's go."

My heart beats wildly as Starr opens the door to exit

her bedroom. This is it! The cool night breeze hits my bare stomach as we tiptoe through the yard and out to the street.

"I told Eddie to meet us in the cemetery," Starr whispers, gesturing to the graveyard down the road. How appropriate that the goth chick lives near a cemetery.

As we reach the wrought-iron gates, car headlights flicker twice in greeting. We scamper over to the parked car, which turns out to be a beat-up red Mustang. Starr hops in the front with Eddie, the driver, and I duck into the back, where Sean is sitting. He smiles at me and places a hand on my knee. Ooh shiver time!

"Hi," he says. "I'm glad you could come."

"So am I," I say, trying not to squirm at the sensation his hand is creating on my knee. He's so yummy it practically hurts.

Eddie revs the motor and soon we're on our way. He turns up the CD player and loud, angry, punk-rock music blares from the speakers, cutting off conversation. Which is fine, actually, considering I'm almost too nervous to breathe, never mind come up with intelligent dialogue.

This is the first time I've ever ridden alone in a car with boys. Pathetic, huh? But The Evil Ones say no car dating 'til I'm sixteen and that's not 'til next month. I'd be so grounded if they knew what I was doing now, it isn't even funny.

But all the potential trouble I'd be in is soon forgotten as Sean reaches over and takes my hand in his. His callused thumb rubs against my palm, evoking a sensation that you wouldn't believe. I swallow hard and concentrate on the raucous, decidedly unromantic music, hoping I can avoid melting into a big soppy puddle on the car floor, which would be way embarrassing.

About ten minutes later, Eddie turns left into the parking lot of a giant warehouse, set back by the river. He parks and the music dies with the motor.

"We're here," he announces. He pulls out a flask from his leather-jacket pocket. "Want a drink?"

Starr frowns. "No way, dude," she says scornfully. "I don't *drink.*" She spits the word out like it's the poison contained in the flask. "Besides the occasional cig, I'm straight edge."

"Yeah, we're straight edge or die, man," Sean agrees from the backseat. "Put that crap away."

I'm not exactly sure what straight edge means, but if it saves me from being asked if I want to get drunk, I'm all for it. I mean even bad-girls-in-training have their limits. And if I showed up at home with even a hint of alcohol on my breath, I'd be sent off to rehab quicker than you can say, "But I only had one sip."

Eddie shrugs, but puts down the flask without taking a swig. Huh. Guess it's like peer pressure in reverse. But hey, whatever works.

We scramble out of the car and lock the doors. Then we head toward the warehouse, Sean again holding my hand. There are dozens of people milling about outside, dressed in bright, candy-colored clothing and smoking cigarettes. Others suck on Blow Pops or pacifiers.

We pay our ten dollars apiece to a pierced and tattooed bouncer type—who surprisingly doesn't ask to see any ID—and head inside.

Flashing lights and pounding techno beats grab hold of

my senses the moment I step through the doors. Everywhere I look there are sweaty bodies moving and gyrating in time to the music. The whole place radiates a kind of energy, almost as if it's alive.

Wow. All I can say is wow.

"Come on, let's dance!" Starr urges, grabbing my free hand. Sean laughs and releases my other hand as I'm dragged away. We head out onto the middle of the warehouse floor.

As the music pounds into my brain, I lose my self-conscious inhibitions and allow myself to be carried away by it all. The techno enters my ears and drips through my entire body until I am alive with the sound and one with the rhythm.

I look around at the other dancers. Some sway slowly to the beat, others dance at an excited pace. There are black kids, white kids, Asian kids, Spanish kids. Ravers, goths, jocks, preps, hippies, stoners. Rich kids, poor kids, kids wearing major bling, kids wearing plastic jewelry. Beautiful, ugly, fat, skinny. All dancing as one, all entranced by the DJ's spell.

It's like in this place no one gives a care about your social standing. The amount of money you have or don't have. Who you are, who you hang with, who you avoid like the plague. When you're here, when you're dancing, this is your family. A family who doesn't ask what grades you get in school. Or what you want to be when you grow up. All that matters to this family is the here and now.

I feel hot breath on the back of my neck and turn around to find Sean behind me. He snakes his hands around my waist and together we trance out to the beat.

SK8ER BOY

You know when you're listening to your iPod and a song comes on that's so beautiful it gives you chills and you want to cry and laugh all at the same time? Dancing with Sean is like that, multiplied by about three thousand. His fingers scorch my bare waist and his eyes set wildfires ablaze in my insides. I'm completely blown away and loving every minute of it.

This has got to be so much better than some candlelit, quiet dinner for two. Better than snuggling by a blazing fire and feeding peeled grapes to one another. Better than walking barefoot down the ocean shore at dusk. Better than any romantic movie cliché you can possibly think of. It's alive and free and brave and wonderful.

After about half an hour of bliss, I realize I'm dying of thirst, all my body's fluids having sweated out of me. I pantomime a drinking motion to Sean. He nods and leads me by the elbow off the crowded dance floor and into a smaller side room. Here, a second DJ spins soothing, chill-out music that greatly contrasts in tempo to what's being played in the main area. Multicolored, fluffy pillows have been strewn across the floor and a juice bar takes up one wall.

We order orange smoothies and retreat to a pillowed corner of the room with our drinks. There are only a few other people around, vegging out, not paying attention to us. I sip my smoothie, rejoicing as the icy relief travels down my parched throat.

"Yum," I say.

Sean stretches out his legs so he's in complete relaxed lounge position. "Yum," he agrees, staring at me in a way that makes me wonder if he's talking about his drink.

He reaches over and brushes a damp lock of hair from my eyes. "You're all sweaty," he says with a teasing glimmer in his eyes.

"Um, yeah," I say, taking in his own shiny face. "Talk about the pot calling the kettle black."

We laugh together. This is so nice. I feel so warm and cozy and happy and content for the first time in my life. Curled up in pillows, next to an uber hottie, snug as a bug in a Berber Carpet rug.

The old Dawn wouldn't be able to enjoy herself here. She'd be too worried that The Evil Ones found out where she was and were on their way down to bust her. But the new Dawn is determined not to worry about things that are out of her control.

"So," Sean says, finishing his smoothie and setting it on the floor. "Tell me about yourself."

I shrug. "There's not much to tell. I'm fifteen. I go to Sacred Mary's and—"

"Wait, I'm not talking your standard four-one-one," he interrupts. "I mean like the real you. What are your goals? Your dreams?"

"Oh." Okay, I know my face is beet red now. I grab a pillow and hug it in my lap. "I don't know."

"Oh, come on," Sean chides. "Everyone has goals and dreams."

"I know, but . . ."

"It's okay. If you don't want to tell me, that's fine," he says kindly. "I just want to get to know you better, that's all."

Ooh, he wants to get to know me. That's a good thing, right? In fact, a very good thing, I should think. All of a sudden I have this undying urge to start spewing verbal vomit like Lindsay Lohan in *Mean Girls* and tell him everything.

At the same time, I'm frightened. I've never told anyone my secret life dream of being a poet/writer. What if he thinks I'm totally dumb and naive? I mean, who makes it as a poet in this day and age? No one even reads poetry anymore. It's not like the old days of Shakespeare. Even Jim Morrison of the Doors had to set his poetry to music before it became commercially successful.

"I'll tell you," I say at last. "But it's kind of stupid. So you have to promise not to laugh."

"Dreams aren't stupid," Sean replies, taking my hand in his. Wow, how can one simple move like that turn me into complete mush? "Though, of course, there are tons of people out there who try to make you believe that. But that's only 'cause they're like, blind sheep, running around with no imaginations."

Wow. He's so deep.

And so . . . right, too. I mean, who gives a care what anyone else thinks of the achievability of my dream? It's mine, after all, not theirs. And if I believe it, if I think I can find a way to make it true, then that's all that really matters, right?

"Okay," I relent. "But you first." Make him put his money where his mouth is.

He grins and pokes me in the ribs with his free hand. "Coward," he teases. "Okay, fine. I have two, actually. My first dream is to become a professional skateboarder. To compete in national competitions and get sponsored by a skateboarding company." He smiles. "You know, like Tony Hawk, only most likely on a much smaller scale."

"That'd be awesome," I say, genuinely impressed. Wow. I can totally picture myself as a pro skater's girlfriend—standing on the sidelines during competitions, cheering on her man. Fielding the jealous stares from all the other girls who wished Sean was with them. . . .

Oops, sorry. This is supposed to be about Sean's dream.

"I mean, I have no idea if I'm even that good," he's saying. "But there's a regional skateboarder competition coming up and I'm gonna enter. The winner gets sponsored by a local skateboard design company and an actual college scholarship." He pauses, his eyes shining. "Which would put me one step closer to achieving my second dream. To be the first in my family to go to college."

"No one in your family's gone to college?" I ask, before I can stop myself.

His eyes fall to the ground, his enthusiasm deflated by my callous question. Nice one, Dawn. "Nope," he says. "Not that we're stupid or anything. But do you know how much college costs these days?"

I have no idea how much colleges cost, namely because cost is not a factor in my household. The most expensive college in the country could not put the merest dent in Dad's bank account. It's so sad to me that someone who actually wants to go to college may not end up going and here I am, not really even wanting to go (at least not to uber-expensive Harvard!) and being forced to by rich parents. Life is so not fair.

"So that's my dream," he says with a small shrug. "Your turn."

"I want to be a poet," I say, deciding to go for broke. "But everyone thinks it's stupid. My dad says I'm wasting my time. My friends think it's completely geeky. But I can't help it. I love poetry. When I'm writing, I can completely block out the world and I feel . . . I don't know . . . alive, or something."

My voice cracks a little at that last bit. Great. Now I'm going to start crying. Which is so not me. In fact, I usually take pride in the fact that I'm not one of those overly dramatic, cry-at-the-drop-of-a-hat girls. And here I am, right in front of Sean, ready to start bawling like a baby.

Lovely.

"I know you can't make a living being a poet," I sniff, trying to compose myself. "And everyone thinks they're a good poet, so maybe I suck. Maybe I'm the worst poet known to mankind and I'm just deluding myself into thinking I have some talent and—"

Sean leans over and shuts me up with a kiss.

•

Chapter Nine

Gah! There's like no buildup. No smoldering glance. No leaning in slowly and wondering which way to turn my face so we don't bump noses. Just BAM! I'm locking lips with Sean.

Can we say OMG?

His lips are soft and taste like orange smoothie, and the chills they spark rocket through my body until I'm almost convinced I'll start shooting fireworks from my fingers and toes any second now. Which sure would be interesting . . .

Sean pulls away a moment later, way too soon for my liking. "Sorry," he says, and I can see he's blushing. How adorable. "You just looked so cute and passionate there, I couldn't help myself."

He is *the* most wonderful boy ever. Possibly the most wonderful boy in the entire universe. I want to marry him and have his babies and grow old and hang out in matching rocking chairs on our front porch watching the young'uns and saying things like, "Back in our day, we didn't behave like these whippersnappers."

Not that I'm going to admit that right now. Don't want the boy to jump up and run from the room screaming.

"It's okay," I say shyly, staring down at my smoothie. "I kind of liked it."

"Yeah? Cool," he says, sounding a bit shy himself. He is so cute I cannot even stand it. "Wanna go dance some more?"

Um, dance? No effing way. I don't want to dance. I want to stay right here and make out with Sean until the sun rises over the horizon. And then continue until it sets and rises again. In fact, I'm pretty convinced if Sean were to kiss me nonstop for the next fifty years, I still wouldn't have my fill of his scrumptious lips.

"Sure," I say out loud. "Let's go dance." 'Cause like I said, I so don't want to scare the guy off. I've got to play my cards right. Not be too easy. Keep him wanting me. Desiring me. At least that's what I read in last month's *Cosmo Girl*.

So we head back on the dance floor. It's late, but I'm even more exuberant than before, the kiss having flooded me with energy. We dance and we laugh and we dance some more. I have no sense of time or place. Just the here and now. The being with Sean. The amazing Sean. Sigh.

"Time to go!"

It seems only minutes later, but has probably been hours when Starr interrupts me with the mandate of returning home before her dad wakes up and finds us gone. Reluctantly, Sean and I follow her and Eddie out of the warehouse. I'm shocked to see that the sun is already peeking over the trees. It's morning and I've been out all night. I've never, ever stayed up all night before, never mind stayed up dancing and making out with a cute boy.

Life is definitely looking up for the Dawnster.

Eddie drives us back to the cemetery. We say our good-byes—Sean gives me the most adorable peck kiss on my nose—and head back to Starr's house.

"That was so amazing," I say, twirling around in the early-morning air, unable to stop babbling. "That was like the best night of my life."

Starr smiles at me and squeezes my shoulder. "I'm glad you had fun," she says. "Sean seems like a really nice guy."

"He is. Really, super nice." I wonder if this means Sean is now my official boyfriend. How delicious. I have a boyfriend. A sexy, wonderful, cool, skateboarder boyfriend. Woot!

A nagging thought tugs at the back of my brain, pestering me with reality crap that I don't want to think about right now. Namely, what will The Evil Ones say about Sean?

One, I'm not even supposed to be dating yet. Not until I turn sixteen next month. And two, even if I did meet their puritanical age prerequisite, Sean's not exactly the type of guy they'll be expecting me to bring home. A bit too diamond-in-the-rough for their tastes, I'd say. And not Brent Baker the Third, whom they've been dying to pimp me out to since my diaper days. In other words, they want me with a guy from a good family who has a mapped-out future like they have for me.

A punk skater from the wrong side of the tracks who may not even go to college is not an option for me, in their eyes. They will so never let me date him. Not in a million years.

But I can't not date him. Not now. I adore him. He's like the best thing ever. I can't bear to lose him just because of their stupid rules. I'll just have to be careful. And then try to figure out how to break it to them eventually.

Like, by sending them the wedding invitation in the mail?

"I can't believe it's morning," I say, glancing at my watch and then releasing a yawn. I'm so tired it's not even funny.

"Yeah, well, I'm totally going to sleep all day," Starr says with a laugh. "Sunshine is way overrated."

"Lucky. I've got to be at the nursing home in two hours for my volunteer work."

"Can't you call in sick?"

"No way." I shake my head. "The Evil Ones would like never let me stay over at your house again if I did that."

And since staying over at her house is the only way I'm going to get to see Sean, I'm so not burning that bridge. No, I'll manage to stay awake. Somehow.

My future with Sean depends on it.

Chapter Ten

"Dawn, dearie, wake up."

"Five more minutes, Mom," I murmur, pulling the covers over my head.

Except there are no covers.

I jerk up and look around. I'm not at home. Not in my bed. In fact, I've evidently fallen asleep in Mrs. McCrery's rocking chair at the Sunnybrook Nursing Home.

"Sorry, Mrs. McCrery. I had kind of a late night last night." I grin ruefully as I reach down to the floor to retrieve the paperback I'd been reading aloud to her.

"It's okay, sweetheart," she coos. Mrs. McCrery doesn't have any living relatives and has taken me on as her adopted granddaughter. I could probably apologize for stealing all her Vicodin and selling it on the black market and she'd forgive me for that, too. (Um, not that I'd do that, obviously.)

I glance over at the sweet-faced woman sitting primly in her nursing-home bed. She's ninety-two and doesn't get out of bed much these days, but always insists the nurses dress her each and every morning. Heaven forbid she be asked to greet guests wearing her nightgown, she always says.

I shouldn't have even come today. I'm so tired I feel sick to my stomach. Working on less than two hours of sleep—bleh! Any reasonable person would have called in sick, but Mrs. McCrery lives for my visits and I couldn't bring myself to disappoint her. One time I skipped a Saturday because of a dance recital and the old woman tried to break out of the nursing home to come find me, convinced I'd been in a deadly car accident—that's what happened to her real-life granddaughter Kelly. It took three days and a special Tuesday visit from me to reassure her I was still alive and kicking. So no matter what else is going on in my life, I have to see Mrs. McCrery.

"Now, where were we?" I ask, flipping the pages of the romance novel I'd brought to read to her. When I first met Mrs. McCrery, the woman liked nothing but long historical epics, which bored me to tears. So now I try to mix it up a bit—broaden her literary horizons, so to speak. Like today; we're reading this way cool action romance about vampires, werewolves, and robots, all living in futuristic LA. And she's totally digging it. Which goes to show, old people can be way cooler than most people assume.

"The good part," Mrs. McCrery crows, clapping her wrinkled hands together. I stifle a groan. By the good part, she means the sex scene. Sometimes I try to skip over those—kind of embarrassing to read out loud to a woman who could be your great-grandmother—but they're her favorite part. And since I've already fallen asleep on the job, I figure I should probably indulge her this time.

"He leaned in to caress her delicate—"

"Do you have a beau, Dawn, dearie?"

I put a finger in the book to hold its place, happy to put the sex-scene reading aside. Evidently Mrs. McCrery has picked up on my just-been-kissed afterglow. I'm not surprised. Even in my exhaustion, I feel I'm radiating nuclear-powered love vibes.

"I'm kind of seeing a guy named Sean," I admit, fiddling with the end of my braid, a soppy smile accompanying my admission.

"Sean. Such a nice Irish name," Mrs. McCrery says with a sigh. "What's his family name?"

Hmm. Actually, I have no idea. Weird. I mean, on one hand I feel like this guy is my soul mate, and on the other, I hardly know anything about him. Where does he live? What's his family like? When's his birthday? The only things I know are that 1) he wants to be a professional skater and go to college, and 2) he's an amazing kisser.

Luckily, with Mrs. McCrery, if you ignore her question for about two minutes, she forgets she's asked it. Which is very helpful, since she tends to ask some pretty embarrassing questions. But while this time she does forget, she also has a follow-up to her initial query.

"What do your parents think?" she asks pointedly. Hmm. Sometimes she can be awfully keen for an old lady.

"They haven't met him yet," I admit. "But I'm sure they'll love him when they do."

Yeah, right. The Evil Ones will take one look at Sean's

scruffy skater appearance and start sending out wedding invitations. Not! They're so pigheaded they'll never give him even the slightest chance to prove he's a good guy.

Meh. The more I think about it, the more I realize how much this whole thing sucks.

"Dawn, may I see you after class?"

A heavy weight plunges to the pit of my stomach at my Chemistry teacher, Sister Mary Anne's, words. The bell rings and all the other carefree, not-in-trouble students file out of the classroom and I, instead, must approach the front of the room. Not good.

It's Monday, and I'm still exhausted from Friday night's adventure. After visiting with Mrs. McCrery Saturday morning, I went straight to my gymnastics meet. I performed horribly. Even fell off the balance beam while doing the simplest turn. My coach was so not happy. In fact, I had to swear my life away that I'd do better next time just to convince her not to call my parents.

Sunday, I went to church with The Evil Ones (fell asleep after the first hymn) and then had to sit through a formal dinner with all their boring old friends and listen to my dad brag about me and my accomplishments. Of course, he doesn't do this to stroke my ego—no way! He just wants them to think he's all "Father of the Year" or some such crap.

The only thing that got me through it all was my never-ending thoughts of Sean. Sean and his awesome kisses, to be precise. Every time I thought of him I got this warm, squishy feeling that made everything else seem halfway tolerable.

But I realize yummy Sean thoughts aren't going to work this time, as I watch Sister Mary Anne slam down Friday's Chemistry exam on her shiny wooden desk. Nope, no fuzzy making-out memories can soften the blow of the big red "F" scribbled at the top.

Can we say, so not good?

"Dawn, is everything okay?" Sister Mary Anne asks, her squeaky voice filled with concern. The kids call her Mary Mouse behind her back. "This isn't like you."

"I'm fine," I mutter, wondering how on earth I'm going to explain this to The Evil Ones. Maybe I can file papers for my emancipation before progress reports come out.

"You're one of my best students," the Sister says, smoothing her hands over her black habit. "I can't understand this."

I wonder what it's like to be a nun. To swear off men for life. I so could not do that. I mean, what a missed opportunity. A waste of a good pair of lips. Maybe Sister Mary Anne has never met the right guy. If she had, I doubt she'd be able to live up to her vows.

"I know. I'm sorry," I say, staring at the dusty hardwood classroom floor. Wow, all the money The Evil Ones pay for tuition and the school can't find a proper janitor.

"Is everything all right at home?"

"Yes," I say, feeling bad for not being able to explain. I know she's genuinely worried about me and that's nice. But how do I tell a nun I didn't study 'cause I'm dating a new boy? She'll so not be able to relate.

The Sister sighs and picks up the test. I watch in amazement as she tears it in half, then in quarters, and flutters the scraps of paper into the trash. I sure didn't see that one coming.

"I'm going to assume this was a fluke," she says. "And I'll allow you to retake the test tomorrow during class. I'm sure you'll be able to get a better grade the next time around?" she asks, raising an eyebrow in question.

Relief floods me. "Definitely. Of course. Thank you, Sister," I babble, practically bowing to her in my relief. This is great. I can go home and study all night. Then tomorrow I'll be able to ace the retest easy. The Evil Ones will never know the difference. Phew.

At that moment, my phone buzzes in my purse. I say a quick good-bye to the nun and dash out of the classroom. As soon as I'm in the hall, I whip out the phone to see who texted me. Hoping upon hope it was Sean.

I'm not disappointed.

>Want 2 come over 2nite?

My heart pounds triple time as I reread the message. He wants me to come over? To his house? That's like a second date. How cool is that? And this time we'll be alone—no Starr and Eddie to interrupt us. Which means plenty of time for kissing. Man, I can't wait to kiss Sean again. I think I'm turning into a nympho or something.

Then my pounding heart sinks as reality kicks in. There's no way I can go over to his house tonight. I've got to study for my Chemistry test. I can't screw up my second chance at a good grade. That'd be suicide.

My phone buzzes a new message.

>My mom wants to meet u.

Aww. He told his mom about me? That's so sweet. He must really, really like me if he wants me to meet his family, right? And I so want to meet them. How can I pass up this opportunity?

You know, I could probably swing by for an hour or so and then just stay up all night and study. I'm sure it'll be fine. I've totally pulled all-nighters before. No big deal.

>*I'd luv to meet ur mom. CU after skool.*

Chapter Eleven

The bus pulls up to the downtown stop and I scamper out, giving the driver a friendly wave as I exit. He grunts in return.

I can't believe I'm here. Alone. Without even Starr to keep me safe. I feel all Dorothy, We're Not in Kansas Anymore. And the craziest thing is no one knows where I am. The Evil Ones think I'm safe at the library, studying. And I didn't see Starr at school to mention it to her.

I look around. Downtown is just as ghetto as I remembered it. Crumbling, boarded-up factories from back when it was a thriving shoemaking town line the street. Squat convenience stores, with bars over the windows and panhandlers by the doors, dot every other corner lot. Lovely.

I involuntarily shiver. You know, I could probably get murdered down here. Knifed or something. And no one would know where to look for my body. Major creepola.

I wonder which missing-girl photo my parents would select for the milk carton, should I disappear. It'd better not be that geeky one from seventh grade. The idea of me, beaming in braces, on milk cartons across the country is way more frightening than my current geographic location.

Picking up my pace, I head down to the parking deck where I'm supposed to meet up with Sean. My pulse speeds up with the anticipation of seeing him again and nervous butterflies torment my stomach. You know, if he keeps having this effect on me, I'm bound to develop some kind of cardiac arrhythmia before I hit twenty. Though at least I'll die happy.

Under the parking deck, I hear him before I can see him. The crashing, echoing of his skateboard as his wheels take flight and then collide with concrete as they descend back to earth.

I catch sight of him shortly after. He's turned a trash barrel on its side and is jumping it with his board. Once airborne, he shifts his body to the right and flips around in the air so he lands facing the other side. Impressive, if you ask me. Très impressive.

I stand back a little, wanting to watch his moves for a moment before making my presence known. Skaters are such talented athletes; it's a shame society doesn't accept their sport as mainstream. At Sacred Mary's, if a guy doesn't play football, he might as well be wearing a big "L" for loser on his chest. But IMO it takes a lot more courage and skill to skateboard than to smack into people wearing tons of padding.

Sean's in midair when he catches sight of me. Recognition lights up his face before the distraction causes him to lose balance and crash to the ground. I gasp as his knee slams into the hard pavement and literally bounces him a few feet.

"You okay?" I ask, running toward him in concern.

He sits up, brushing himself off. The fall has torn his pants, leaving a gaping hole in the knee and I can see blood underneath. "Yeah, I'm good," he says. Boys. They always have to be so Vin Diesel.

"You're bleeding," I say, kneeling down to check his battle wound—a big bloody raspberry. "I may have a Band-Aid in my purse. . . ."

He laughs. "My little Florence Nightingale," he teases. "I don't need a Band-Aid. I just need you to kiss it better."

I look down at the bloody mass. "You want me to kiss . . . that?" I ask, a little hesitantly. I mean, I like the guy and all, but eewww.

He cracks up and takes my head in his hands. "No, silly. I hurt my lips."

I don't see as much as a scratch on his full, beautiful mouth, but who am I to argue? Giggling, I lean in for a smooch. His lips are soft and warm and his breath its usual peppermint fresh. As he kisses me, he runs his hands through my hair, evoking chills down my backside. I shiver in delight and press my mouth harder against his. I am so growing to like this whole kissing business.

"I missed you," he says as we part lips.

"I missed you, too," I say. It's hard to believe I last saw him early Saturday morning after the rave. Only two days ago. It feels like a lifetime.

"So, you want to go meet Mrs. McNally?"

I scrunch my eyebrows. "Who?"

"Aka Mom."

"Oh!" I laugh at my confusion. At least now I know Sean's last name. "Sure. If you're done skating."

"Yeah. I'm good." He scrambles to his feet and pops up his skateboard so he's now holding it in his hand. "I was just screwing around until you got here."

"What was that trick you did over the barrel?" I ask as we walk out from under the parking deck. "That was way cool."

"It's technically called a Frontside Ollie one-eighty," he says. "Which basically means you jump and then do a hundred-and-eighty-degree turn so when you land, you're backwards."

"Oh. Cool," I say. "Sorry, I wish I knew more about skateboarding."

"That's okay. I wish I knew more about poetry," he replies. "And I hope you'll let me read yours someday."

He wants to read my poetry? Wow. He is way too good to be true. I mean, what boy would want to read poetry? Like, willingly, without being required to in school?

He leads me up a steep hill and turns right at a crumbling monument. I look around at the neighborhood, a little nervously. It's real bad. Again, like major ghetto-ish. Narrow streets lined by decrepit old apartment buildings with peeling paint and trash-filled front yards. Mangy pit bulls growl behind chain-link fences. Two guys in a corner alley talk in low voices and I see one pass something to the other in the most secret of ways.

"Oh my God." I nudge Sean. "I think they might be dealing drugs," I whisper. I've never seen an actual, real-life drug deal before. I wonder if I should get my can of pepper spray out of my purse, just in case.

"Just ignore them," Sean says, as if it's no big deal. As if that kind of thing happens all the time. And maybe it does in this neighborhood.

The wind picks up, whirling debris around the street. A piece of paper blows into my leg and I pick it off gingerly, hoping it doesn't have any weird germs on it.

"Who's she?" I ask as we turn the corner. I watch as a heavy-set woman in a red wig and gold miniskirt parades the sidewalk, waving at cars. Julia Roberts, *Pretty Woman*, she is not.

Sean frowns and turns to look at me. "Where did you say you lived again?" he asks.

"Um, East Oaks," I say, feeling a little ashamed for some reason.

"You live in East Oaks?" he asks. His voice is as incredulous as if I just told him I turn into a green ogre every night à la Princess Fiona in *Shrek*. What's up with that? "I mean, I knew you went to Sacred Mary's, but I had no idea that . . ." He trails off, shaking his head. "I figured you lived over near Starr or something."

"So I live in East Oaks." I shrug. "What difference does it make?"

"Maybe this wasn't such a good idea."

"Why not? Of course it is. I want to meet your mother," I protest.

Great. I'm once again stereotyped 'cause my stupid parents have more money than God. Like I asked to be born into their family. Last I remember, babies don't get much of a choice whose pregnant belly they get beamed into.

"Okay. Fine," he says, running a hand through his curly blond hair. "We're almost there."

I fall in step silently, cursing my big mouth. Why did I have to act all suburban nightmare around him? Shocked by a drug deal. A prostitute. Who am I? Heidi on the mountaintop with her grandfather and goats? I'm acting like such a pampered princess all of a sudden. If Starr were here, I'd definitely earn back the Barbie nickname at this point. *Stupid, Dawn. Real stupid.*

Sean stops in front of a two-story gray apartment building with a rotted-out front porch. "Home sweet home," he says sarcastically, climbing up the steps. "Don't say I didn't warn you."

Gone is the sweet, cute voice he normally uses with me. In its place I hear a weary sarcasm, laced with defensiveness. Not good. I want to reassure him somehow that I'm not here to judge his lifestyle. That I like him for who he is, not what he has, but I'm afraid if I say anything else, he'll revoke my visitation rights altogether.

He yanks open the squeaky, rusted screen door to the left and we head inside the first-floor apartment. My nostrils fill with a warm, spicy smell, mixed with something that's a bit too ripe. We walk through a darkened hallway and into a small living room with sunken, ripped couches and peeling wallpaper. A bearded twenty-something with dreadlocked brown hair sits sprawled on one sofa, glazed eyes staring at the old television set in the corner. He has a beer in one hand and a cigarette in the other.

"Hey, Turd, did you bring me my cigs?" the guy calls, not taking his eyes off the television.

Sean rolls his eyes, but reaches into his pocket and tosses a soft pack of Marlboros at him. The guy looks up to catch them and his eyes fall on me. He misses the cigs.

"Ooh, who's this little succulent suburban?" he asks with a lecherous leer.

"Shut up," Sean says automatically, leading me by the elbow into the next room. "Don't pay any attention to him," he says loud enough for the guy to hear him. "That's my loser brother Jerry. He's under house arrest for selling weed. See that device on his ankle?" We turn and he points to Jerry's lower leg. "If he leaves the house, it alerts the police."

OMG. Sean's brother is a criminal? Under house arrest? I swallow hard. What have I gotten myself into? I take a deep breath. *Be cool, Dawn. It's no big deal.*

Yeah, right. It's a huge big deal. My parents would kill me if they knew I was here. I mean, I gathered Sean wasn't exactly rich, but I had no idea he had *America's Most Wanted* living in his house. I am never, ever going to be allowed to date this guy. Ever. The Evil Ones will send me to a nunnery, fit me for a chastity belt, and ground me for a millennium before they let me date Sean.

This sucks.

We head into a tiny kitchen/dining area combo where a short woman with graying black hair and a plump, rosy face is stirring something on the stove. She's wearing a faded pink housedress that doesn't do much to hide her rotund figure. Must be Sean's mother, though I don't see much resemblance between her and the tall, thin skater. She turns from the stove as she hears us enter.

"Sean!" she cries joyfully, planting a sloppy kiss on his cheek. He kisses her back. "And you must be Dawn," she says turning to take me in. "She's so pretty, Sean!" She pulls me into a big, squishy embrace. She's so soft, it feels kind of nice. Nothing like my bony mother's half-hugs.

"Mom, this is Dawn. Dawn, Mrs. McNally, my mother," Sean says, a little wearily.

"It's so nice to meet you, Dawn," Mrs. McNally exclaims, releasing me from my hug. "Sean has told me so much about you."

I suppress a guilty grimace. Sean's had actual convos about me with his mother? And here I haven't even told my parents we're dating. Does this mean I'm a really bad girlfriend?

"Are you hungry?" Mrs. McNally asks, sizing me up. "Would you like some dinner? You're so skinny. Just like my Sean."

I glance over to Sean, who seems a bit mortified, so I hurry to jump in.

"I'd love something to eat, Mrs. McNally," I say.

She claps her hands together in delight. "Oh, good. I was hoping you'd say that. I made enough food to feed an army." She giggles. "Then again, we have an army to feed, so that's a good thing. Sean, go call your brothers and sisters."

I soon realize she's not kidding when she says she has an army. At Sean's call, half a dozen kids and teens of various ages swarm the tiny dining room and find their places at the table. It's amazing they all fit, but somehow they do, albeit a bit squished. I can't believe so many peo-ple live in this tiny apartment.

I take my seat beside Sean and dig in.

The menu is simple, spaghetti and meatballs, but deli-cious. At dinner, the McNally family fight and laugh and argue. Even occasionally threaten to throw food at one another. I think about the formal, elegant dinners my par-ents subject me to on a nightly basis. Their indignation when I spill a miniscule drop of food on the pristine white tablecloth. They'd be horrified at the noise and the mess of this supper. But I love it. It's so full of life. So refresh-ingly different from what I'm used to. I'd love to have a family like this—have sisters and brothers to tease and be teased by. A mother who laughs and doesn't judge or condemn.

But just as I'm starting to relax and enjoy myself, the questions start.

"So do you live around here, Dawn?" asks Patti, Sean's fifteen-year-old sister. She tosses her long brown hair over one shoulder. "I don't think I've seen you at Woodbury."

"I actually go to Sacred Mary's," I mumble. Here we go.

"And she lives in East Oaks," Sean chimes in, his voice laced with sarcasm. I glance over at him, hurt. What is his deal? He's supposed to be on my side.

"Oh, wow. East Oaks!" Susan, the twelve-year-old, exclaims. "I love those houses. They're so huge. Do you have a pool? Do you have servants?"

Sean's fork makes a squeaking noise as it scrapes against his plate. I bite my lower lip, wanting to crawl under the table and die of embarrassment. I know if I answer the affirmative I'll only make things worse. But then again, it doesn't seem fair that I should have to lie. Why should he make me feel embarrassed about my life? It's not like I chose it.

"Well, we have a housekeeper named Magda," I say carefully. "Though she's more a member of the family than a servant."

"Ha! A member of the family who slaves away in the kitchen and does all the laundry," snorts Jerry, the jailbird. "I wish I had one of those."

"You do," teases Ben, Patti's twin. "She's called Mom."

"And you don't even have to pay her!" Susan adds with a giggle.

I think my cheeks are going to melt off my body, they're burning so bad. Why did I have to open my big mouth? Of course I'm not going to be able to explain to them that I really care about Magda. That she's the one I turn to when The Evil Ones are driving me crazy. That she's like a second mother to me. They'd never understand.

"Not Magda Rodriguez?" Sean's mom pipes in, effectively taking control of the conversation from her rambunctious children.

"Uh, yeah, that's her," I say, cocking my head at her. "How do you . . . ?"

"I figured," Mrs. McNally says, nodding. "She told me she's been working for some rich family up in East Oaks. She lives down the street from us. You know the blue house on the corner of Elm Street, Sean? That's where Magda and her children live."

Sean stares at his plate and doesn't answer. He looks

mortified. And why shouldn't he be? We've just established that my family's servant is his family's neighbor. Not like it should make a difference, but I know it does. To him, at least.

The conversation turns and I'm off the hook. But Sean barely says a word during dinner, just shovels pasta into his scowling mouth. I've barely taken my last bite when he suggests he drive me home. Like he can't wait to get rid of me.

Gah, this hurts.

After saying goodbye to the McNally clan and promising to come back and visit soon, we exit the house and climb into his battered Ford pickup truck.

"I love your family," I say, hoping to put him at ease. He inserts the key in the ignition, still not looking at me, and the truck sputters to life. I persist. "Your mom, especially. She's so nice."

Sean doesn't answer. He throws the car into gear and pulls out, staring ahead at the road.

I can't believe this is the same guy who danced with me at the rave. Who told me dreams are never stupid. Who wanted to read my poetry. He was so warm and sweet and cool then. What the heck happened?

Not being able to bear the cold-shoulder treatment, I decide to call him on the carpet. "Okay, dude. You were completely silent all through dinner. What's wrong?"

"You don't have to patronize me," he says at last, in a tight voice.

"What?" I ask, genuinely taken aback.

"I know what my family's like. You don't have to pretend you're all cool with it."

Huh? What's he talking about? I mean, I know the money thing is bugging him, but his family?

"But I'm telling you I loved them," I say, confused. "They're so lively and fun. They're great. I wish I had brothers and sisters."

His frown deepens. "Yeah. You think it's cute. You can go slumming. See how the other half lives. Then you return to your East Oaks mansion and laugh to your friends about your Adventures in White Trash. Like, oh so *ghetto fabulous*," he says in a mocking tone.

I stare at him, horrified and hurt. "How can you say that?" I ask, swallowing hard to keep from crying. "I'm nothing like that."

"No?" Sean's frown twists into a grimace. "Okay, then. When we get to your house, invite me in."

"Wha-what?"

Sean nods as if he's proven some point. "Exactly. You won't invite me in 'cause you're ashamed to tell your parents about me."

"I'm not—"

"You are. In fact, I'm willing to bet my skateboard you haven't even told them you're seeing me. And that if you did tell them, they would ground you for all eternity."

God, how do I argue with him when he's hitting the nail on the head? But this is so not my fault. It's not me and what I think, it's them.

"How about my mother asks your mother over for tea?" Sean says, continuing his tirade. "You think your mom would come by and hang out with mine? 'Cause I can have my mother call her tomorrow and set up a date. Maybe she could meet my convict brother while she's at it."

I can't breathe. I seriously can't breathe.

"Sean, please don't—" I beg, tears streaming down my cheeks.

"Face it, Dawn. This isn't going to work. You're a cute girl, but we live in two different worlds."

"It doesn't matter," I sob, desperate to get a word in. "We're not defined by our parents. We could make this work. I really like you."

"You like me now. I'm a novelty. I'm different from the other guys in your neighborhood. I'm dangerous and by dating me you can rebel against your parents. But think about the long-term, Dawn. Seriously." He pulls up to a red light and turns to look at me. I drop my eyes, unable to face his angry, hurt expression. "It can't go anywhere. You have a brilliant future ahead of you. And I have nothing."

The light turns green and he pulls forward. We enter the East Oaks subdivision and I direct him to my house. My big, ugly mansion with its stupid front-yard light-up fountain. I've always thought it was pretty. Now I think it's horrible, ostentatious. Embarrassing.

Sean pulls up at the bottom of the driveway and kills the engine. He turns to me, taking my hand in his.

"I like you, Dawn," he says, his voice calm and earnest. "Don't get me wrong. But I know the realities here better than you do."

"Please don't do this," I beg, all pride forgotten.

He sighs deeply. "Do you want me to come up and meet your parents? Right now?"

A stab of panicked fear punctures my heart. If he comes up now, my parents will know I've disobeyed and lied to them. Broken every one of their rules. And they'll hate Sean tenfold because of it. I want them to meet him. Badly. But not like this. He's never going to understand that, though. I break into fresh tears. He's going to take my "no" answer as a personal judgment against him and his family's bank account.

Sean nods knowingly. "I thought so," he says slowly. "It's okay, Dawn. Stop crying. I get it." He releases my hand. "Now go inside before you get in more trouble."

I don't want to leave his truck because I know this good-bye is going to be forever. The cutest, nicest, most wonderful guy I've ever met and I've already lost him. All because of my parents. They really deserve the name The Evil Ones.

I swallow hard, trying to salvage some sort of pride. "Good-bye, Sean," I say, forcing my eyes to meet his sad gaze. "I'll miss you."

He leans over and gives me a small kiss on the cheek. His lips burn my tear-streaked skin. "Good-bye, Dawn," he says.

And with that, I get out of the truck and slam the door behind me. He revs the engine and pulls away. I stare after his truck, pressing my fingers to my cheek. The cheek he just kissed good-bye.

I hate my life.

Chapter Twelve

I open the front door to my house, desperately trying to mask how upset I am. I so don't want The Evil Ones to see me crying. They'll ask why and then I'll have to make up some stupid excuse.

"Dawn? Is that you?" asks my mother, lounging on her couch in our icy parlor. If she were Sean's mom, she'd probably get up from her seat to greet me. Wrap me in a warm hug and ask how my day was. But no; to my mother, I'm not even worthy of the calories it would take to stand up.

"Yeah, it's me," I mumble as I start upstairs. I don't want to have to face them. Not with my blotchy, tear-stained face.

"What are you doing home? I thought you were at the library."

I stop dead in my tracks. Shoot. I was so upset I forgot I was supposed to have Sean drop me off at the library, not home, to make my lie believable.

"I, um, took a cab home," I fib. One good thing about having Sean break up with me is I can stop the web of lies. It's exhausting to keep track of them all.

"You took a cab?" Dad roars from his armchair. "Dawn, get in here. Now."

Oh, freaking great. I back down the stairs and drag my feet into the parlor.

"What?" I ask defensively, even though I know exactly why he's pissed. I should have said one of the Ashleys dropped me home, as usual.

"You know very well what," Dad rages. "We don't want you taking public transportation. It's dangerous. And anyway, you don't need to. We could have picked you up. All you had to do was call us."

"What, you want to send a limo after me or something?" I yell back, unable to control myself. I'm already at my breaking point, and I'm so not ready to deal with his stupid public-transportation crap.

"What limo? What are you talking about?"

"Or, I know. Send poor Magda. You make her do everything else around here!"

My mother stares at me, disbelief written across her face. "She works here, Dawn. It's her job."

"Yeah, well, did you ever consider her feelings? That maybe she doesn't *want* to slave away in the kitchen for ungrateful rich people and then have to go play chauffeur?"

"She's not a slave, Dawn. She chooses to work for us. And we pay her very well for her services," Dad says.

"What is all this about?" my mother asks. "Has Magda said something to you?"

"I'm going to have a word with her," Dad adds. "If she's unhappy here . . ."

"No. Wait. Magda didn't say anything," I cry. Oh, great. On top of everything else, now I'm endangering Magda's job. I love Magda, no matter what Sean's family thinks, and I can't be the one who gets her fired. I think quickly. "I'm just . . . in history we're studying class differences in Regency England and I'm a little sensitive to the rights of the servant class right now."

Wow, I pulled that one from my butt, huh? And just in the nick of time, too. I may not enjoy lying, but I'm darned good at it, if I do say so myself.

Dad settles back in his armchair, still looking a bit grouchy. "It's nice to see you caring about those less fortunate than you," he says. "But how about channeling that noble energy into less dangerous ventures than taking cabs so your housekeeper can slack off? You can volunteer to do charity work, if you're interested. I'm sure it would look great on your Harvard application."

Oh, yeah. Just what I need. More time suckage. Then again, now that I have no life once again, I'll probably have plenty of time to fit it in.

"Sure, yeah. Whatever," I mutter. "I've got homework." I turn out of the room and head upstairs. Whew. That was way too close. If they hadn't been distracted by the whole Magda thing, I'm sure they would have launched into a game of twenty questions about whether I was actually at the library.

I get to my room and slam the door shut. I hate them. Their little, pathetic, judgmental lives. How I'm forced to be one of them. Their captive prisoner.

They didn't even notice I'd so obviously been crying. Or

if they did, they didn't bother to bring it up. Too busy yelling at me for breaking their stupid rules to ask if I'm okay.

You know, I can't wait 'til my eighteenth birthday; the moment I blow out those birthday candles, I'm taking off. Never to be heard from again. I'll get some cool little apartment downtown and find a job, like a good, honest, hard-working person, and live a normal, happy life.

Like Sean.

I sigh as I crawl into my bed and absently twist my belly button ring as I stare at the ceiling. I miss him already.

The tears start flowing again and this time I don't bother to stop them. Why did things have to turn out like this? Just because of my stupid parents. And my grandparents who made all that money before them. I so didn't ask to be rich. I don't want to be. Especially not at this price.

I know I need to study for my Chemistry make-up test, but what's the use? Who cares whether I do well or not? Maybe if I flunk out of school, my parents will realize I'm not cut out for their perfect little Ivy League nightmare. That will teach them a lesson for trying to ruin my life. Maybe then they'll start leaving me alone.

I reach my arm out from under the covers to grab my purse. I pull out my cell phone and flip through Sean's old text messages. The ones I couldn't bear to delete. A lump forms in my throat as I read through each one. They're all I have left to remind me of our brief but wonderful relationship. I never even took any photos.

I toss the phone aside and curl up into the fetal position under the covers, wishing the pain would go away.

Chapter Thirteen

I wake up the next morning feeling like I've run a mental marathon. I could barely sleep and I'm exhausted. When I did pass out for a few brief moments, I had crazy dreams where Sean comes back, carrying a big bouquet of roses. Begs for my forgiveness. Says our parents' bank accounts don't matter. That he loves me and can't bear not to be with me forever and ever.

And then I'd wake up and realize it'd all been a dream. And that's when the tears would come, again and again. It's amazing how many tears your body can produce. They say our bodies are made out of like eighty percent water and I'm quite certain I bawled out at least sixty-five percent last night.

Thank goodness there's a rain storm and crew practice is canceled due to the lightning and thunder. I don't think I could have forced myself to expend the energy it would have taken. So I lie in bed a few extra moments and then get up to get dressed for school.

I should have called in sick. I feel sick. Sick with disappointment. In English class, I can't concentrate on anything the teacher is blabbing on about. Something about Hamlet's girlfriend Ophelia, going crazy and committing suicide 'cause the selfish jerk dumped her.

Ophelia, I totally sympathize, girl.

I open my notebook and start writing. Poems start pouring out of me to the point that it's kind of scary. My pen can't even keep up with my ideas. Of course every one of them is about Sean in some direct or indirect way. About our doomed relationship, ended too soon.

At lunchtime I head to the caf and scan the room for Starr. I have to talk to her about Sean. She's the only one who's in on our relationship. The only one who will understand and maybe know what I should do.

But my punk-rock friend is nowhere to be seen. Weird. I head over to the table where she normally sits and greet Sophie and Stuart.

"Hi, guys," I say with a friendly smile.

They look up, both regarding me with cool eyes. "Hi," Stuart says, then pauses. "Um, what?" he asks, in a totally sarcastic Why Are You Here Bothering Us tone.

Okay, then.

"Uh, have you seen Starr?" I stammer. Why are they giving me the cold shoulder all of a sudden? After all, I was their hero earlier in the week, when I told off the Ashleys.

"Haven't you heard?" Sophie asks, her big green eyes wide and sad.

"Heard what?"

"Starr got expelled for showing up to school drunk," Stuart butts in. "She's going to Woodbury from now on."

My heart sinks. My world spins off its axis. I can't

believe this is happening. Starr got expelled? She's going to public school? Why would she show up to school drunk?

"Oh, God. I have to talk to her," I say, rummaging through my purse for my cell phone. "Make sure she's okay."

"Her dad took away her phone," Sophie adds. "And she's grounded for like eternity. No visitors."

"Gah! That's not possible. I need to talk to her," I cry.

"Sucks to be you, then," Stuart says, digging back into his food. Sophie slaps him on the arm.

"You're so rude," she whispers, giggling.

"Well, I mean, come on," he whispers back.

"Uh? I'm still standing here," I remind them, more than a bit ticked off. What is their problem?

They both look back up at me. "Oh, yeah. You are, aren't you," Stuart notes in an ironic tone. "Though I don't understand why, *Barbie*."

His words sting and I turn around and flee the table before they can see my tears. After all the Sean stuff, my nerves are already shot and their ridicule is really the last straw. I glance back to see the two of them giggling together.

Revenge of the nerds.

I wipe my eyes with my sleeve, looking around the caf. Okay, now what? Starr's gone. And Stuart and Sophie won't let me sit with them if she's not around.

Maybe the Ashleys will forgive me.

Swallowing hard, I walk over to the other side of the caf and find my three former best friends at their usual table. Except they're not alone.

Some other random girl is sitting in my seat.

"Um, hi!" I cry as I approach them, forcing my voice to sound chipper. "How are you guys?"

All four girls look up, almost in sync, and regard me with perfectly shaped raised eyebrows.

"Well, look what the cat dragged in," Ashley #1 says, giving me the once-over.

Oh dear. This is not sounding good. I knew this would happen. Why did I even try? Do I have a humiliation wish or something today?

"So guys, I've got a great lunch poll," I exclaim cheerfully, giving it one last shot. "If you had a thousand dollars and could only buy one purse, what would you choose?"

"My purse costs more than a thousand dollars," sniffs Ashley #2.

"I know where *you'd* buy one, Dawn—a thrift store," Ashley #3 snarks off. "Or maybe Salvation Army. 'Cause you're like so alternative now."

"Prada, definitely," Ashley #1 chimes in. She's unable to help herself when it comes to fashion polls. The other two Ashleys turn and stare at her. "Uh, I mean," she stammers, "your mother!"

Okay, then. That made no sense. But I get the point loud and clear. I'm not going to be welcomed back into their fold.

"Whatever," I say, sounding more confident and nasty than I feel. "I was going to give you guys another chance, but forget it."

I storm away before they can respond. As soon as I leave the caf, I start running down the hall. Tears half blind me and my braids whip against my neck. I can feel people's stares and know I probably look like a possessed freak, but I don't care.

I reach the bathroom and enter a stall. I sit down, using the toilet as a chair. It's the only place I can think of that I can cry unobserved. I'm totally Lindsay Lohan in *Mean Girls*, except I'm so not bringing my lunch tray in here. I mean, ew.

I'm such an idiot. Such an idiot. I threw away my best friends in the whole world to hang around with some stupid girl and get involved with some stupid guy and now both of them are gone and I'm left with nothing. Nothing!

High school is going to suck from now on. I'll have no friends to hang out with. I won't be invited to anything cool. For the next two years I'm going to be a social leper.

Why, Dawn? Why did you get yourself into this mess?

I don't blame the Ashleys at all. I publicly dissed them. Called them losers. Skanks. After years of friendship, I blew them off like the top of a fluffy dandelion. They hadn't ever done anything wrong to me. Tricked me. Hurt me. Talked behind my back. (At least as far as I know.)

But I had to be cool. I had to impress Starr and her friends. Make them see I wasn't a Barbie. And so I told off my best friends in the world. Publicly humiliated them.

I'm so stupid. So, so stupid.

Wait a second. In my self-torturing I almost forgot about Starr. But now Stuart's words come flashing back at me. Expelled! For drinking! But Starr doesn't drink. I remember when Eddie offered her a flask before the rave. She flat-out refused and said she was straight edge or die.

I hope she's okay.

I exit the bathroom stall and splash cold water on my face, staring at my blotchy reflection in the cloudy mirror. It's so obvious I've been crying. But whatever. Who gives a care anymore?

I wander the halls for the rest of lunch period, my stomach growling in protest. But I can't go back in there. Wander around the caf, wondering where I now fall in the high-school social circle. Because I'm too afraid of the answer: nowhere. I'm no longer one of the populars and the so-called losers have rejected me as well. I'm like stuck in this weird void where I practically don't even exist.

The bell rings, thankfully, and I duck into my D period class. Chemistry. Oh, goody. Now I get to fail my make-up test, too. Talk about adding a cherry on top of my already crap sundae of a day.

I start to sit down, then think better of it. Oh, screw this. I know I won't be able to pass the test, so why bother taking it? Maybe if I don't show up to class, Sister Mary Anne will let me reschedule it for tomorrow instead.

I leave the classroom and cut through the library. There's a back door in the library. A back door out of the school. And it's got my name written all over it.

Chapter Fourteen

It's funny. A week ago I never would have considered skipping out of school. I mean even if trench-coated kids showed up with Uzis, I'd probably ask for a pass first. I was such a goody two-shoes.

Now I'm an exhausted, jaded outcast who's flunking out of school. And I've got to get out of here.

I manage to leave school grounds without being spotted and catch the bus downtown, all Girl on a Mission. I slouch in my seat, feeling very juvenile delinquent, not that the bus driver cares. When we reach my stop, I jump out, this time not bothering to wave good-bye.

I head up the street and soon the town's public high school, Woodbury, looms before me. I wonder if I should walk through the front doors or find some side entrance. I wonder how I'm going to find Starr in a school of thousands. I wonder if my Catholic-school-girl outfit is going to make me stick out like a sore thumb. I bite my lower lip. This wasn't a very well-thought-out plan.

I decide the front door is still my best bet. Just walk through with confidence, as if I own the place. I ditch my rosary beads in the bushes and pull my shirt from my skirt and tie the shirttails together, revealing a little belly skin. Now I look less uniformish, at least.

I step through the front door and am shocked at how big the school is. The hallways are wide with high ceilings. Lockers line every inch of wall space. A bell rings and suddenly I find myself caught up in a wave of high schoolers pooling down the hallways.

"Smells Like Teen Spirit," as that old band Nirvana would have said.

"What are you doing here, Dawn?"

Augh. I whirl around, my heart in my throat. In my worry about Starr, I'd totally forgotten the fact that Sean goes to Woodbury, too. But there he is, standing in front of me, looking oh-so-adorable in his button-down surfer shirt and khaki shorts. Gah, I missed him. Even though I just saw him yesterday. I want to collapse in his arms and sob and cry and beg him to come back to me.

Of course I don't. I mean, that would be relationship suicide. If I have any hope of getting him back (which I'm pretty sure I don't, but whatever!) I have to play it cool. So even though my hands are shaking like I have Parkinson's and I can barely speak, I manage to throw him a casual oh-how-nice-to-see-you smile.

"Hey, Sean."

He scratches his head, still staring at me. OMG, I hope he doesn't think I'm like stalking him or something. Like that movie *Swimfan* where the guy has sex with the girl in the pool and then she goes and ruins his life. That would be way too embarrassing.

"I, um, forgot you went here," I stammer.

"But you don't," he says pointedly. Oh man, he really does think I'm Stalker Girl.

A wave of hallway salmon swimming upstream push by us, shoving me into him, and for a moment I'm in his arms as he reaches out to catch me. I rejoice in the feeling of his hands on my forearms. I'll never wash this shirt again.

"Come on, it's too crowded here," he says. He leads me down the hallway and we duck into an empty classroom. He flicks on the light and closes the door behind him.

I wander over to a desk and slump down. "You think I'm, like, stalking you, don't you?" I ask mournfully.

He chuckles and props himself on the desk in front of me. "Well, if you are, it'd definitely be a first for me."

Yeah, right. He probably gets stalked all the time. I mean, look at him. He's so gorgeous. So wonderful. Probably every girl in Woodbury is obsessed with him. He probably has *them* carry *his* books to class.

"Well, I'm not," I insist. Might as well put all my cards on the table. "I came here to find Starr."

He scrunches his adorable face. "But Starr goes to Sacred Mary's. . . ."

"Did go," I correct. I explain what I know about Starr getting drunk, getting expelled, now attending Woodbury. How I'm worried about her and how I need to see her to make sure she's all right, since they took away her cell and I can't reach her any other way.

"Wow," Sean says, looking as concerned as I feel. "So you skipped out of school to come find her?"

I nod glumly. "Though I have no idea how I'm going to do that in a school this big."

Sean thinks for a moment. Then he jumps from his desk and heads over to the classroom computer. "I know," he says. "Come here."

I follow him over and watch as he sits down in front of the computer and starts typing. I have no idea what he's up to—the screen is complete gibberish to me.

"Um, what are you doing?"

"I'm hacking into the class schedules," he says. "They tell you what students are in which class. So we can find out where she is."

"You can . . . hack?" I ask, shocked.

"Sure. My mom was always too poor to pay for a good computer when I was a kid, so I built my own from spare parts I found in the garbage outside this electronics store," Sean explains. "And taught myself how to get free Internet access and stuff."

Interesting. I had no idea just how talented this boy was. I only saw him as a cute skater, when really there's so much more to him. He must be totally smart to hack a computer. I can barely figure out Microsoft Word.

"Here we are," Sean says, before I can comment further. I lean in to focus on his pointing finger. "She's in Room 203, Algebra."

"Cool! Thanks!" I cry. He turns around quickly and we bump noses. Kind of Eskimo kiss. How can he not feel the sparks flying between us? "Uh, sorry," I say, not really meaning it.

"It's okay," he says, rising from his seat. "Let's go."

I raise an eyebrow. He wants to come with? I figured he'd be ditching me right about now. Coolio.

" 'Kay," I say, trying not to sound too delighted.

We exit the classroom and hang a left and then take a flight of stairs up to the second floor. The second bell has rung and so all the kids are in class, making the hallways easier to navigate. But still, I'm glad Sean's with me on my secret mission. I'd be completely lost in this maze of a school without him. Plus I like the tingle in my body his close proximity causes. Not that I should be thinking about that, but I can't help it.

"This is it," Sean says, pointing to a closed classroom door. "Room 203."

I surreptitiously peek through the small window and see Starr sitting in the back of the classroom, a scowl on her face.

"She's in there," I whisper-squeak to Sean. "Now what? Do we wait for her to come out?"

"Class just started. You'd have a long wait," he replies.

"Oh. Well, that sucks."

"Nah, here's what you do," Sean says. "You walk into class like you own the place, right? And then you say you're here from Guidance and Starr needs to report to the Guidance Counselor immediately."

I look at him. "And that'll work?"

"Yup." He nods confidently. "Guaranteed. They send student messengers all the time. Guess 'cause they don't want to use the intercom during class and interrupt everyone."

"Wow. The nuns at Sacred Mary's would never fall for that one," I say. "But okay."

I take a deep breath and wrap my hand around the

doorknob. I wonder what will happen if I'm busted. Will they call and report me to my school or just kick me out of Woodbury? Will Sean get in trouble for being with me?

I pull open the door and step into the classroom, concentrating on looking both confident and bored. "Um, like, hi?" I address the teacher, using my best dumb blond voice. "The Guidance Counselor wants to see Starr—er . . . Ashleigh down in her office? Like immediately?"

Out of the corner of my eye I can see Starr staring at me. She looks shocked. I swallow a smile.

"Okay," the teacher agrees, without missing a beat or looking the least bit suspicious. "Ashleigh?"

Four girls stand up.

"Uh, Ashleigh Robinson," I clarify.

Three sit down. Starr makes her way to the front of the classroom.

"Thank you, sir," I say to the teacher. Then I turn and walk toward the exit.

Once outside, we reclose the classroom door. Sean beams at me. "Good job," he says.

"What the heck are you doing here?" Starr demands, looking rather pleased to see me.

"Shhh," I say. "Let's go somewhere we can talk."

We head back downstairs. Sean suggests we hit the auditorium, which is only used during after-school drama practice. Sure enough, when we arrive, the place is deserted. We plop down on the stage.

"So, you going to tell me what you're doing here now?" Starr asks again.

I laugh. "It's actually more fun keeping you in suspense, but okay." I stretch out my legs on the floor. "I wanted to make sure you were okay. I mean, one day you're at Sacred Mary's and the next you've been transferred. And Stuart and Sophie said you were grounded and that your dad took away your phone. So, like, I figured the only way to find you was to come to school."

"But why aren't you in school yourself?"

"I was. I left."

Starr stares at me, openmouthed. "You left?"

I giggle. "Yeah. I snuck out."

Starr raises her hand in a high five. "Wow, girl. You rock." We slap hands. "But really," she says in a more serious tone. "You shouldn't have risked getting in trouble. Not to come see me." She nods her head toward Sean. "Though I guess you got a two-for-one deal by coming here."

My face grows hot at her teasing remark. I forgot she has no idea that Sean and I broke up. I glance over at the skater in question and he's as red-faced as I probably am.

"Actually, Sean and I aren't together anymore," I say, using my bravest voice. "So I just came here to see you."

"You broke up?" Starr stares at the two of us. "But then . . . ? What are you . . . ?"

"Starr, this is not about me and Sean. This is about you. They told me you got expelled for showing up to school drunk. You don't drink. You're straight edge. What happened?"

Starr sighs and turns her gaze toward the ceiling. "I know. I'm a total loser, huh?"

I frown. "No. You're not. There's obviously got to be some reason. So, like, what's going on with you?"

She lies down on her back, still staring skyward. I remember her in this position one other time. When she started telling me about her mother.

"Oh," I say, suddenly realizing. That's got to be it.

"One year ago yesterday was the day my mother died," Starr confirms, her voice kind of choking out her words. "I woke up and I . . . I just couldn't deal with it. I missed her so badly." The tears start flowing from her eyes, smearing her mascara so she looks like a miserable, rabid raccoon. "I loved her so much, Dawn. She was like my best friend as well as my mom. We used to do everything together before she got sick."

My heart breaks for Starr. I can't imagine what it must be like to lose a parent. It'd turn anyone's world upside down. And here I am complaining about how much my life sucks and really all my parents do is set boundaries they feel will keep me safe. I mean, yeah, they are completely overprotective, but they're doing it because they love me.

"I'm sorry, sweetie," I say, reaching over to stroke her hand. She squeezes her fingers around mine.

"Anyway, I asked my dad if I had to go to school and he said yes. He never talks about her. Or her death. It's like he wishes she never existed," Starr says. She wipes at her tears with her sleeve. "So I was mad and I raided his liquor cabinet and drank half a bottle of bourbon." She makes a face. "Nasty stuff. Really gross. I don't recommend it.

"I felt okay when I got on the school bus. But I think our bus driver must have been a former racer in the Indy 500 or something 'cause he drove like a bat out of hell.

By the time I got to school, I was totally nauseated." She groans. "So I'm like, desperately seeking a bathroom, when Sister Frances stops me in the hall and asks me if I'm okay. I guess I looked a little green. I tried to answer, but it all came out puke. I totally hurled all over her."

"Ew, dude, you ralphed on a nun?" Sean exclaims, sounding grossed out and impressed all at the same time. "That's so effed up."

"Yeah, no doubt," Starr says, sitting back up. "And for a nun, she's no dummy. She figures out exactly what's going on and hauls me into my dad's office. At first I think, like, he's going to give me some light sentence 'cause he knows the circumstances, but no. He says I have to set an example and I've embarrassed him from the moment he enrolled me in Sacred Mary's. Et cetera, Et cetera. So he says he's sending me to Woodbury. As if that's some bad punishment. I would so much rather be here anyway than that stuck-up richie private school."

"Well, I'm glad you're okay," I venture. "I was really worried about you."

Starr smiles. "You're sweet, Barbie," she says.

I make a face. "You're not going to start calling me that again, are you?"

"Sorry." Starr laughs. "You're right. Your Barbie days are over." She scrambles to her feet. "But anyway, no need to worry about me. I'm fine. I'm digging the open-mindedness Woodbury has to offer. There are way more cool people and more interesting classes to take. I fit in so much better than at Sacred Mary's. So tell the gang I said hi, and if I ever get off my groundation life sentence, I'll see you around." She starts to leave, then turns back to me. "And thank you, Dawn," she says in a more serious tone. "It really means a lot that you cared enough to come find me."

And with that, she saunters out of the auditorium, leaving Sean and me alone.

"Well, that solves that mystery, I guess," I say. "I'm glad she's okay."

"I still can't believe you snuck out of school to come check on her," Sean says. "That was so cool of you."

I shrug. "I guess," I say, trying to sound nonchalant. But inside I'm doing the Snoopy dance. Sean's paying me compliments. He's seeing me as something besides poor little rich girl. That can't be a bad thing.

"Listen, I've got to get back to class," he says, his voice actually sounding reluctant. As if he'd prefer to stay here with me. "And you should definitely get back to Sacred Mary's so you don't get into worse trouble."

"Yeah," I say. I know he's right. If I get back now, there's still a chance I can fake that I was in the nurse's office or something and not get in trouble for missing my make-up test. But still . . . I steal a glance at Sean. I don't want to leave him. Chances are after this I'll never see him again and—

"Can you meet me after school?" he asks quietly. "Down by the parking deck? I want to talk to you."

Hope surges through me at his words. He wants to talk. That's got to be a good thing, right? If he didn't want to get back together, why would he ask to see me?

"Sure, I guess," I say in my utmost casual voice. "See you after school."

We jump up from the auditorium floor and part company. Me through the doors out of the school and him through the hallways to class.

I am so glad this good-bye is the "see you later" type.

Chapter Fifteen

You know, I should skip school more often. I don't think anyone even realized I was gone. Major woot!! And anyway, even if they did, it was so worth it.

I head to my last period Honors History class with a big smile on my face. I can't wait to meet with Sean after school. I wonder what he's going to say to me. I just know he's going to ask me back out, don't you think? I mean, there's no other possible explanation for why he'd want to see me.

I daydream through the rest of my day and when the bell rings, I skip out of school and catch the bus downtown. I'm so good at this public transportation thing now. And the downtown neighborhood doesn't even freak me out anymore. In fact, it seems almost comforting. Like no matter what's going on in my crazy life, this weird world's always there to greet me.

I'm still a little worried about Starr. I mean, she seemed okay and I'm glad she likes her new school, but . . . well, she's definitely got some issues she needs to work out in the home-life department. Issues she seems to have swept under the rug. I hope I can be there for her, to help her through it all. But in the end, she's got to deal with her own demons, I guess.

I arrive at the parking deck and listen for the banging of skateboards. But there's nothing. Just silence. I must have beat them all here.

I head down to my normal spot and see Sean sitting on the curb. I wave. He doesn't have his skateboard with him. I wonder why.

"Hi," he says, smiling at my approach.

"Hi."

He pats the curb, inviting me to sit down. I squat down beside him, trying to resist the thrill that spirals though me as we bump knees. Why does he have to be so yummy?

"Sorry to make you come down here," he says. "But I wanted to talk to you. And school didn't seem the right place. Not when some teacher could walk in at any moment and bust us."

"Totally," I agree, bobbing my head. "Especially since I don't even go there. They'd probably, like, arrest me for trespassing or something."

"I know you have things you have to do after school, so I'll be quick," he adds.

"Oh, no, actually I'm free this afternoon," I lie breezily. Truthfully, I'm skipping ballet and the teacher is bound to inform The Evil Ones. But I don't care anymore. I really don't. Sean is way more important to me than some stupid dance class. Way more important to me than my stupid parents' rules. In fact, if he were to ask me to drop out of school and run away to join the circus, I'd run home and pack.

"Oh. Okay, cool." Sean grabs a stone off the ground and tosses it from one hand to another. Fidgeting. He looks nervous. Whatever he has to tell me must be big.

"It was really nice of you, coming to find Starr today," he begins, tossing the rock at the curb opposite us. It bounces off the cement and lands a foot away.

I shrug, trying to remain casual. "Yeah, again, no biggie. Just wanted to make sure she was okay. I mean, anyone would have done the same thing in my place."

"Not really," Sean insists. "Most people, I've found, wouldn't give a crap." He pauses, staring at the ground. "You're, like, a really good person," he says, mumbling his compliment a little. "Nothing like . . ." He trails off, getting up to grab the rock he'd thrown and then sitting back down.

I look over at him, studying his hesitant face. I have no idea who he's talking about, but I can tell the Big Admission Into the Past section of the program is coming right up.

"Nothing like who?" I ask.

He sighs and throws the rock again. "You know how I freaked about you living in East Oaks?"

You mean the time you broke my heart by basically calling me a spoiled little rich girl who was using you as a white-trash novelty to rebel against my parents' totalitarian rule?

Um, not like I'd forget that one.

I nod in response.

"Well, two years ago, I met this girl. She was really pretty, like you. Very sweet. Or so I thought. She was from East Oaks, too, and I was madly in love with her."

Okay then. A little TMI on the "madly in love" part, but I'll let it slide this once. After all, he did, however indirectly, just tell me he thinks I'm pretty.

"We knew each other from school—she went to Woodbury, too—so we sort of dated a while before I thought to ask her to come home and meet my mom," Sean says. "And when I did, well, this girl took one look at my house and my family and totally freaked. She was out the door and into the arms of some rich dude from her neighborhood before you could say 'bling bling.'"

I nod, afraid to speak. Now this is all making perfect sense. No wonder he'd acted as he had.

"My mom kept asking where she was," Sean goes on. "Why she didn't come around after the first time." He smiles a little. "Well, you've met my mom, you know what she's like. She loves people and loves to be around them. And so of course the last thing I wanted to do was hurt her by telling her what the girl had said." He pauses, and when he speaks again his voice is laced with hurt and regret. "The girl I trusted. The girl I was in love with and brought over to my house. She called my mom a fat, white-trash cow."

I can't help it. "What a bee-yotch!"

"Yeah." Sean exhales a deep breath. "I mean, we're poor, sure. But we're actually doing okay, you know? My mother always figures out a way to make sure we're all fed, even though my deadbeat of a dad hasn't contributed two cents in the last ten years. At times this means working three jobs. But she does it—she sacrifices everything for us. And she never complains."

My heart literally aches for Sean and his family and how they've worked so hard to have so little. I'm so selfish and spoiled—always whining about my life when I've never even had to lift a finger.

"So for this girl to waltz into our lives and judge us . . . well, it hurt . . . you know?" He shakes his head. "So anyhow I didn't want anyone coming in and hurting my mother's feelings again. Making her feel like she's a bad mother. 'Cause she's the best," he adds, his voice shaking in his fierce pride. He turns back to face me, his blue eyes wide and sad. "When I found out you were from East Oaks, I completely freaked. I was so afraid you were going to react the way my ex did. And even when you didn't, I kept wondering if you were thinking it all and were just too polite to come right out and say it. So I flipped out on you. And you totally didn't deserve it."

He reaches over and takes my hand in his. I can't even breathe at this point.

"I'm sorry, Dawn," he says, his eyes searching my face for acceptance. "I judged you the same way I didn't want you to judge me. For how much money you had, not what kind of person you are."

"It's okay," I squeak, my voice not working as well as I'd like it to at the moment. "I understand."

He squeezes my hand so tightly, it practically hurts. "Thank you," he says. "You're a good person."

He leans in closer and I suck in a breath, knowing what's coming. I close my eyes and find his mouth by touch. His kiss is soft at first, his lips feather-light as they explore mine. Then the kiss deepens in intensity, evoking a strange fluttery feeling down to my toes.

He's back. The Sean I love is back. And he's accepted me for who I am, just as I accept him for who he is.

I'm so happy I want to cry. Or laugh. Or just kiss him a lot. A real lot.

Suddenly a car's screeching brakes interrupt this moment of tenderness and passion between us. We break the kiss and look up, only to see a BMW squeal out of the parking lot. My heart stops beating for a split second as I catch the license.

I'd know that vanity plate anywhere.

ASHLEY1

As in Ashley #1, former friend, and now sworn enemy. As in Ashley #1, child of The Evil Ones' best friends, the Parkers. As in the best friends who play bridge with The Evil Ones every Thursday night.

As in tonight.

Ashley #1 has just seen me making out with a boy under the parking deck on the wrong side of town.

I'm so dead.

Chapter Sixteen

"What's wrong?"

Of course Sean notices something's wrong. I'm quite positive every last drop of blood has drained from my face and I'd currently make Casper the Friendly Ghost look tanned.

I motion to the spot where the BMW pulled out moments before. "That car belonged to my ex-friend Ashley," I say. "And I'd be willing to wager my entire college fund that she's on her way to tell her parents she saw me with you."

"And let me guess," Sean fills in. "You all go to the same country club."

I grimace, but nod. "Yeah. The Evil Ones are bound to find out about us by nightfall."

Sean drops my hand. "I didn't want to get you in trouble. . . ."

"Oh, no!" I assure him. "You didn't. This was my decision to come down here. Sean, I want to be with you. And I'm not going to let my parents run my life anymore. You're not some dirty little secret I have to hide. If they don't approve of us, well, that's their problem to deal with. Not ours."

"Oh yeah?" Sean asks, cocking his head in question. "You sure about this?"

"Yup." I nod enthusiastically. "As sure as I am that Brad Pitt is hot. Er—" Don't want to give him the wrong impression "—sure as I am that Jessica Simpson is an airhead?" Darn it, why does my mind always blank on good analogies? "That Paris Hilton won't run out of money? That Mary Kate Olsen doesn't need to diet?" Ugh, these are getting worse and worse.

He laughs and gives me a happy smooch on my cheek. Gah! Even his quick pecks have the power to send those crazy tingles to my toes and fingertips. If he could market that kind of electricity, he could solve the energy crisis.

Suddenly, a perfect "sure as" analogy comes to me. At first I'm not positive I should say it. Get it out in the open like this. It's risky, but it's true, and, well, I'm sick of playing games and following the rigid dating rules from the editors at *Seventeen*.

"As sure as I am that I love you?" I say, then hold my breath as I wait for his response.

He smiles widely and pulls me into a warm hug, his fingers stroking my back. "You know, Dawn?" he whispers, his breath in my ear evoking a billion more tinglies. "You should say, as sure as you are that *I* love *you*."

"Oh really?" I nuzzle my face into his shoulder. Feeling happier at this moment than I can ever remember feeling my entire life. "*Am* I sure about that?"

"You should be."

* * *

I open my front door like I'm dead girl walking, ready to face my executioners. At the same time, my insides are breaking out the nonalcoholic champagne and dancing on tabletops. It's a bad combo of feelings and it's making me a little sick to my stomach, to tell you the truth.

"Dawn Ashley Miller! Get in here. Now!"

I cringe. Here we go. Put the Sean Loves Me celebration on ice. The Evil Ones have arrived to bust up the party.

I drop my book bag and turn into the parlor. Mom and Dad have actually expended the calories needed to rise from their seats and are currently staring at me, arms folded across their chests and extreme fury in their eyes.

Gulp.

"Hey, guys," I say, in an inane attempt to pretend nothing's wrong. "How's it hangin'?"

"Sit," my dad says.

Uh, yeah. Woof, woof, Dad. Are you going to give me a Scooby Snack afterwards?

I plunk down on the hard antique sofa, wondering how anyone in this century or last could actually think it was comfortable. I mean if it's worth money, fine. Sell it on craigslist and then hit Pottery Barn. No need to keep it around, cluttering up your house and offending the poor butts that have to sit on it.

"What is going on with you, young lady?" Mom starts in first.

"What do you mean?" I ask, channeling that wide-eyed, innocent look of Puss in Boots in *Shrek 2*.

"Cut the bull, Dawn!" Dad storms, evidently channeling his inner ogre. "We just got off the phone with Ashley Parker's parents."

I swallow hard. I already figured that they must have, but to hear it confirmed still kinda stung. Thanks a lot, Ashley. Good friend you turned out to be. Then again, she probably phrased it in a way that made it seem like she was only looking out for my safety. Bee-yotch.

"And your Chemistry teacher," my mother adds.

Oh, oh. I squirm in my seat. At this point even a Pottery Barn sofa would seem mighty uncomfy.

This is worse than I thought. I mean, I figured I could talk my way out of the Ashley thing—maybe say it was a case of mistaken identity or something, but if Sister Mary Anne narced on me, I'm screwed.

". . . and your gymnastics coach. And your ballet teacher. And the yearbook advisor," Dad lists off.

Crap. Crap, crap, crap!

"Do you want to tell us what's going on?" Mom asks, in her pseudo shrink voice.

"Not especially," I mutter.

Dad explodes. His face is beet red, his nostrils flaring. "Failing tests? Skipping school? Ditching after-school activities I pay good money for?"

I really have no defense for any of this, so I just sit there, staring at my hands, waiting for it to be over. My stomach burns in anger and I want to punch a wall or something. It's that frustrating. You know, anyone who says being a bad girl is all fun and games should get her head examined.

"And if all that's not enough," Dad rages. "Then we find out from Ashley Parker you've been sneaking off to a dangerous part of town and are cavorting publicly with some white-trash crackhead underneath a parking deck.

Dawn, what's going on with you? We didn't raise you to act like this!"

Okay, that's it. I leap from my seat, squeezing my hands into fists. They can yell at me, they can call me on the carpet about my failings in school, but they're not going to insult poor, sweet, innocent Sean who did absolutely nothing wrong.

"He's not a crackhead!" I yell, giving Dad the most evil glare I can muster. If only I were Medusa and could turn him into stone with just one look. "You don't even know him!"

"Dawn, you're not even allowed to be dating yet," my mother pipes in with her stupid logical argument. "Not until your sixteenth birthday."

I turn on her. "Of course I'm not allowed to date yet. I'm not allowed to do *anything* yet. My whole life is one big 'no.' Every day filled to the brim with a series of activities I have no interest in. That you've forced upon me against my will."

"Dawn, these activities are important," Dad interjects. "Harvard requires that prospective students—"

"Screw Harvard!" I cry, staring him down with my hands planted on my hips, totally in unleash-the-fury mode. "I've never wanted to go there anyway. It's a stupid school with a bunch of elitist snobs. It's your dream that I turn into some Ivy League nightmare, Dad, not mine! It's never been mine."

I didn't think it was possible for someone to be so red in the face as my dad is now. I'm a bit worried about his heart condition, but I can't stop.

"You know what *my* dream is, Dad?" I demand. "No,

that's right, you don't. You don't know anything about me. What I want to do. Who I want to be. 'Cause you don't give a rat's butt. As long as you can brag to your friends that your daughter's following in her old man's footsteps, that's enough for you. I'm like a stupid puppet for your ego."

"Dawn, that's not—" Mom tries.

"Not what? Not true? Yes, it is, and you know it. Okay, then. What do I want to be when I grow up? Huh, Mom? If you're so keyed into Dawn's life, tell me."

My mother shrugs, looking defeated.

Of course.

"Yeah, I thought so," I reply. I push past her and storm out into the hallway. "Let me guess. I'm grounded for the next two millenniums. I'll be up in my room." I stomp halfway up the stairs, then stop and turn to face them.

"By the way?" I add in my sweetest voice, then pause for dramatic effect. "I got my belly button pierced too."

I have to admit, the horrified looks on their faces does give me some satisfaction.

Chapter Seventeen

If I thought my life was boring before, it's ten thousand gazillion times worse now. No phone. No Internet. No TV. No cell. Even the extra-curricular activities I moaned and groaned about have been stripped away.

"Give you more time to work on your little limericks," my father says sarcastically. Yeah. Way to encourage your child to follow her dreams, Dad.

So I wake up, go to school, come directly home, and study in my room. I do not pass go or collect two hundred dollars. In fact, my allowance has been taken away altogether. I'm let out of jail free briefly for dinner and then sent straight back to my room to finish studying.

Once a week I'm also forced to pay a visit to a psychiatrist, Dr. Drugs. (No, not his real name, though that'd be pretty funny. It's more his philosophy. Have a problem? Pop more pills.) He keeps suggesting we consider my taking Prozac. I keep adamantly refusing. I've decided I'm so not becoming a permanent resident of Prozac Nation.

The grounding is set to last for two months. But I'm

not allowed to see Sean again, ever. We're totally Romeo and Juliet now. Well, without the messy suicide part.

And that's the suckiest part. The rest I can deal with. But Sean, I miss dreadfully. I can't even call him to let him know I'm okay. The Vile Evil Ones of Broken Dreams (I've added on to their nickname to better emphasize their true demonic qualities) took away my cell phone and I had his number stored in my address book, so I can't even phone him from a pay phone at school. He's probably totally worried about me.

At least I kind of hope he is. I hope he hasn't gone off with some other girl who's actually allowed to date him. I mean, he's a seventeen-year-old, majorly attractive, super smart Chad Michael Murray lookalike with a killer personality. Some lucky, pretty girl is certain to snatch him up. Why should he wait around for me? I mean, sure he said he loved me, but love can fade in time. And a lot of time is passing.

Seeing as I have hours and hours with nothing to do but think, this worry pops up a great deal. In fact, even asleep I'm tortured in my dreams by Sean cheating on me. Though technically, we were never officially going out, were we? So does that really count as cheating? Well, it sucks either way.

I have to see him again. Tell him I'll be back in two months. That I love him and can't live without him. That somehow, some way, I'll convince my parents he's not a bad guy and I should be allowed to date him. I have absolutely no freaking clue how I'll accomplish such a change in The Vile Evil Ones of Broken Dreams' Grinchsized hearts, but I have to try. My future with the boy I love depends on it.

I roll over onto my back and stare at the ceiling. Why, oh why, did I have to alienate the Ashleys? If I hadn't, then Ashley #1 would have never told on me and I'd still be with Sean. Stupid, Dawn. Real stupid.

"Are you hungry, *chica*?"

I sit up in bed as my door creaks open. Magda pops her head in. "I made your favorite," she says, entering the room carrying a tray piled high with food. "Carne Asada."

My mouth waters. Carne Asada is like this Mexican marinated steak and it's sooo good. We hardly ever have it 'cause of my dad's high cholesterol and my mom's aversion to the fat content of red meat. (I wish she'd switch to Atkins.)

"Yum. What's the occasion?"

She sets the tray down on my nightstand and sits on the side of my bed. She's such a small woman that the mattress hardly bows under her slight weight. "Your parents are out at a business awards dinner," she explains with a sparkle in her dark eyes. "I am your jailer tonight."

I laugh. "Cool." I grab the fork and knife and dig in. It's delicious. Spicy and tender. Magda is a rocking cook. "Can I sneak out then?"

The housekeeper shakes her head. "You want to get me fired?" she asks. "My children would not thank you for that."

Darn. But yeah, I'd never endanger her job. That would be way selfish of me. But the children thing . . . that reminds me!

"Hey, Magda, do you know the McNally family? They live down the street from you."

The housekeeper nods. "Rhonda McNally is a dear friend. She has had a difficult life, raising all those children by herself, but she has managed nicely." She pauses for a moment, then turns to look at me. "How is it that you know them? Surely none of her children go to your school. . . ."

"Her son Sean is my boyfriend," I explain, getting a tingle inside as I say his name. I miss him so much.

Magda raises an eyebrow. "Your parents know about this?"

"Um, yeah. Sort of. Note the groundation."

"Ah," Magda nods knowingly. "Now it becomes clear to me."

I flop down on my bed and moan. "What's clear is how much it sucks, Magda. I totally love him. And he loves me. He told me, last time I saw him. And he's so cute and nice and fun and talented and wonderful. . . ."

"And smart," Magda adds. "That boy has always been smart. I remember the day we caught him running around the neighborhood, still in diapers. He'd managed to figure out the mechanical workings of his crib and escaped like some sort of bambino Houdini."

I giggle, trying to picture the tall, handsome skater as a baby in diapers. He'd probably be so embarrassed if he knew Magda was telling me this.

"Yes, he's smart," I agree. "He is a computer genius, too."

"And very handsome," Magda adds, a teasing glint in

her eyes. "My daughter, she is only eight, and she claims she will marry him someday."

I can feel myself blushing. "Yes, very handsome," I say, with a deep sigh. "Very handsome." I roll over to my side, propping my head up with my hand. "But The Evil Ones see none of this. They think 'cause his family isn't rich that he's not right for me."

Magda shakes her head. "You should not call your parents such names," she scolds. "They are doing what they think is best for you. They love you very much."

"They don't. They love the idea of me. To brag to their friends. And when I don't live up to their ridiculous expectations, they punish me."

"It may seem this way to you," Magda says. "But as a mother of three, I can tell you, it is not so. They look at you and want to do right by you. But they are also scared. They are afraid you will go down the wrong path."

"But Sean's not the wrong path," I protest. "He's totally right for me."

"Is your relationship with Sean the real reason you are grounded?" the housekeeper asks pointedly.

I ponder this a moment. "Well," I admit grudgingly, "I guess I kind of disobeyed every rule in the book, too. But that's only because I knew they wouldn't allow me to see Sean in the first place."

Magda nods. "You will never know, then, will you? Perhaps they would have liked Sean, had you brought him to dinner in the first place instead of sneaking around in dangerous parts of town behind their backs. Lying to them."

Grr. I hate to admit it, but she has a total point. What if I had been honest from the start? Asked him to dinner, introduced him to The Evil Ones. He's so nice and charming, perhaps they would have welcomed him with open arms.

Like Magda said, now I'll never know.

"*Chica*, do not worry so," Magda says, rising from the bed. "Things will work out in the end, I promise. But you should always tell your parents the truth. And know they are not out to ruin your life."

"Yeah, yeah." I sit up in bed to take another bite of my delicious dinner. Suddenly, a brilliant idea comes to me. "Hey, can you do me a favor?" I ask, my mouth full of steak.

"Of course."

"Can you deliver a note to Sean for me? Drop it by his house or something? I can't contact him 'cause they took away my phone and stuff. But I just want to let him know I'm okay." I give her my best pleading look. "After all, even prisoners are allowed to send and receive mail."

"You are too much." Magda smiles indulgently. "Okay, I think that can be arranged. But do not tell your parents."

Yes! I let out a "woot" of joy and jump out of bed to grab a pen and paper. Let them take my cell phone, my IM, my e-mail, my texting capabilities. Let them deny me my right to technology.

The mail, via my rocking housekeeper/friend, will always get through.

Chapter Eighteen

The return note from Sean comes the next day. Scribbled on a scrap of yellow lined paper, folded, and neatly placed underneath my dinner tray, courtesy of Magda.

Dear Dawn,

Whad up? How are u? Probably sucky, huh? That totally blows that u got in trouble with "The Evil Ones." (heh heh!) L Parents. U can't live without 'em and u can't shoot 'em. Ha! Ha! (That's what my brother Larry always says!)

I've been okay, I guess. School's way boring, but I'm gearing up for that big sk8er competition I told u about. U know, the one that offers the scholarship? Yikes! Wish me luck, I'm gonna majorly need it.

Anyway, gotta get to school. My mom says hi and hopes u can come visit soon. She says she'll cook her world famous jambalaya coz u told her how much u luv spicy food!

Okay, talk soon. Don't worry about me. When u get out, I'll be here. I love u and miss u. xoxoox

Love,
Sean

PS Your poems rock! I bet you'll totally be a famous poet someday. Thanx for sharing them with me.☺

I reread the words a thousand billion times and go to sleep with the note under my pillow. He misses me. He's waiting for me. How wonderful is that? Knowing he's there, thinking about me, makes the whole grounding torture seem almost bearable.

And he likes my poems! I had felt a little silly including a few of my favorite poems in my letter, but he had said he wanted to read them, so I figured, why not? With Sean, I figure, I can be myself. The real me.

Man, I had no idea it was even humanly possible to love someone so much. I cannot *wait* to see him again. Stupid Evil Ones, keeping him away.

Two more weeks pass uneventfully. Every day is pretty much the same. At least I'm able to catch up on my schoolwork and the gnawing guilt of falling behind fades away, replaced with an almost satisfying feeling of accomplishment. I mean, call me a goody two-shoes nerd, but I totally prefer having the nuns praise me for my efforts, rather than scold me for my failings. I guess I'm not cut out to be a bad girl, huh? Oh well. It was fun while it lasted.

My social life is still rather dismal, but I'm getting by. I don't know if Starr said anything to Stuart and Sophie or what, but they've invited me back into their little lunch circle, so at least I have people to sit with now. And they're cool. Funny, smart. Interesting. Not into fashion conversations. Sure, Stuart can be bitingly sarcastic and bitter at times, but Sophie usually puts him in his place pretty quickly. It's cute. They're just friends, but they act like an old married couple sometimes.

At first, the Ashleys think it's fun to torture me, and make fun of me, my new friends, my lack of social standing at Sacred Mary's. But when I don't get riled up at their bullying, they get bored quickly, and eventually find new targets to torment. I've come to terms with the fact that I'll never be prom queen or homecoming queen or Christmas queen or any sort of high school royalty now, but I don't mind so much. I've realized there's a lot more to life than just high school.

I'm in my room studying for an English test one Friday afternoon, when my mom enters my bedroom. No knock, of course.

"Hi, sweetie," she says, sitting on the corner of the bed.

I raise an eyebrow suspiciously. Sweetie? To what do I owe *that* term of endearment?

"How's the homework going?" she asks.

"Fine." FYI, I'm still only speaking to my jailers in one-word sentences. They hate it, which makes it all the more satisfying.

My mother sighs and runs a hand through her shiny black hair. She's still beautiful from her modeling days, but her mouth is now lined from too much frowning and a few silver hairs weave through the black strands.

She'd probably say she got them from having to deal with me.

"That's good," she says at last. "Because we're going out."

I raise an eyebrow. "Out? But I'm grounded." Shoot, that was four words. Monosyllabic talking is a lot harder than it sounds.

"Not this afternoon," she says, rising from the bed. "We're going shopping."

I'd probably fall over in shock if I wasn't already sitting down. My mother wants to take me shopping? Has she been replaced by one of the pod people? Become a Stepford Wife?

Too bizarre.

But I am not one to look a get-out-of-groundation-free gift horse in the mouth, even if it is just going shopping with an Evil One, so I slip on my shoes and jump into her Beammer.

We drive to the mall and spend an hour or so wandering through the shops. At first I'm totally dragging my feet, wondering why the heck we're here, but after a bit, I loosen up and start to grudgingly enjoy myself. After all, I haven't seen civilization for two weeks, besides school, which, of course, doesn't count. The lights, the music, the racks and racks of clothing are enough to make me almost giddy with freedom.

"That looks adorable," my mother says as I exit the dressing room wearing a pink Juicy Couture track suit. "I'd like to buy that for you."

I'm not quite sure that pink Juicy Couture track suits fit in with my new image—I see myself more as a Hot

Topic kind of chick now—but my mother looks so pleased, I decide to cut her some slack. I can always wear it to the gym.

We make our purchases (she buys herself some boring old Ann Taylor something or other) and then head to the food court for a snack. My mother again surprises me by getting a hamburger and fries. She hardly ever eats red meat, and I've never seen her order anything fried. But hey, if she's going to do it, I might as well, too. I get mine with extra onions.

"So," my mother says, after a few bites of burger. She picks up her napkin and pats her thin lips. "I heard about the little nickname you have for your dad and me."

I almost choke on my burger. *Man, Ashley, did you have to tell them everything?*

I should have stayed grounded in my room. There's always a cost for freedom.

"The Evil Ones," my mother says, forming each word slowly and carefully. Then she sighs, her expression rueful and hurt. "Do you really think that we're evil, Dawn?"

I hang my head and concentrate on shoveling fries into my mouth. What am I supposed to say? Yes, I think you're evil and you've ruined my life? That would definitely officially signal the end of Take Your Daughter to the Mall day.

"It's just a joke," I mutter. "It wasn't meant to be taken literally."

"I wonder." My mother has another bite of burger. It's so weird to see the Queen of Lettuce chowing on fast food. "Dawn, I know we've pushed you. Maybe too hard at times, but we've always had your best interests in mind."

I snort. Yeah, right. What's best for me is to be able to see the boy I love and not have her judge him on his family's social standing.

All of a sudden, I'm so ready for this shopping trip and forced mother-daughter bonding to be over. What does she think? She can win me back by plying me with clothes and food? Make me think she's cool? This is bigger than a burger. Bigger than Juicy Couture even.

"It's fine, Mom. Whatever," I say, pushing my tray away. I'm no longer hungry. "I won't call you A Vile Evil One of Broken Dreams anymore, I promise."

My mother's face falls and for a moment I feel bad. But still, what am I supposed to say? "I know you have a better idea of how I should live my life than I do, so let me stop and listen to you without question and follow you like a dumb sheep"?

I don't think so.

"It's funny, Dawn," she says at last. "I see a lot of me in you. Especially lately."

Yeah, right. I am nothing like her. Nothing. She's a beautiful, successful model who married the rich guy and lived happily ever after in a sleepy New England town. I am, well, not. Not beautiful. Not successful. Not a model. And certainly not interested in rich guys or sleepy New England towns.

My mother picks a crumb from her burger and rolls it around on the pads of her fingertips. Wow. She's fidgeting. My mother never fidgets.

"When I was your age," she begins in a slow voice, "I was living in New Jersey with my parents, going to public school like any fifteen-year-old. But I was so bored. I wanted something bigger. Better. So I fell in with this biker gang two towns away. I started hanging out with them—smoking, drinking. Met a guy who seemed so dangerous and cool. . . ."

I raise my eyebrows. I'm trying not to be interested, but man, this is juicy stuff. My perfect, elegant mother has a past. Who'd a thunk it? I figured she slid out of the womb perfect—never even giving Grandma labor pains—then glided through life on a silver cloud, picking up modeling gigs on the way and then later that rich husband of hers. I so cannot picture her as a drunk biker chick with a bad-boy boyfriend. It boggles the mind, let me tell you.

My mom pauses, pressing a hand to the side of her face and I wonder what she's implying with the gesture. "Let's just say . . . he, um, wasn't as cool as I thought, but was more dangerous than I imagined."

Ouch.

"You think we control your life too much," Mom continues. "Well, my parents were the opposite. They didn't get involved at all. I could be flunking out of school or be getting straight A's, it didn't matter. As the youngest of ten children, I wasn't even a blip on your grandpa and grandma's radar. They couldn't wait to get me out of the house so they could buy that RV and hit the road. And they certainly didn't want to waste good gas money on a college fund.

"So I ran away to New York to become a model." She shakes her head. "If you want to talk about shady characters, look no further than the modeling business. The agent I worked with was a crook. He stole all my earnings and left the country. I had no money to pay rent. Not even enough for a few packets of Ramen noodles. I called my parents to ask if I could have a small loan." She grimaces. "They had moved away without telling me. No forwarding address either."

Wow. That's so harsh! I try to imagine my mother, homeless and starving on the streets of New York, but I can't. For a moment, I wonder if she's making it all up. To give me one of those Lessons with a capital "L." But after another glance at her red blotchy face, I realize she's not. The story she's telling me is real, and it still upsets her to this day.

Plus it kinda solves the mystery of why I've never met Grandma and Grandpa. . . .

"Why'd you never tell me any of this?" I ask.

My mother shrugs. "I wanted to be a good role model. I wanted you to look up to me." She clears her throat. "And anyway, that part of my life is over. I don't like looking back on it."

I nod slowly. This has got to be the weirdest conversation I've ever had with my mother. Probably weirder than the time she tried to give me the old sex talk before giving up, red-faced, and handing me the "Birds and the Bees and Me" book to read myself after I asked if she and Dad still did it and when. (Hey, I was a curious child!)

"So, Dawn, I guess what I'm saying is, I'm sorry if I've erred on the side of caring too much for you. Pushing you too hard to achieve. But I only do it because I love you so much. Because I want you to have a better life than I had. Any head start possible for a blissful, happy future without hardship.

"I got lucky," she says, brushing an actual tear from her eye. I don't think I've ever seen my mom cry before. It freaks me out a little. "I met your father. He showed me the meaning of love. Of respect. Of caring. And I want you to have that, too."

Okay. We're encroaching on "ew" territory here. Ix-nay on the "how much I love your dad" eech-spay, please.

"At your age, a dangerous boy from the wrong side of the tracks probably seems very appealing," Mom goes on. "But when you get older, Dawn, you'll learn that looks and personality only go so far. Men will try to charm you, but you need to look to the future. Can they provide for you? Offer you the lifestyle you deserve?"

Aha! Didn't I tell you she'd be sneaking in that Lesson with a capital "L"? We've come full circle now and she honestly believes she can exploit her miserable teen years to lecture me about mine.

I'm so not having this.

"Mom, I'm fifteen," I argue. "I'm not ready to 'settle down,' as you put it. I just want to date people." Of course, when I say "people" I mean "person," and by "person" I really mean Sean. But that's TMI for her at this point. I've got to be somewhat diplomatic here.

My mom stares at me for a minute, and I get the uncomfortable sensation an antelope must get right before it's pounced on by a lion. Like I've walked right into her trap.

"All right," she says, a little too cheerfully, especially after her big sob story. Where'd those tears go?

"All right?" I ask.

"Yes. All right. If you honestly think you're ready to date, then I don't have a problem with that."

"Really?" I stare at her, mouth open. She doesn't have a problem with me dating? I'm allowed to date? There's got to be some kind of catch here. She's looking way too smug.

I wait, still the antelope. Then the lion pounces.

"Really," she agrees. "In fact, I think you should start dating right away. So tomorrow night I've set you up on a date with Brent Baker." She smiles sweetly, completely innocent, but I see triumph in her eyes. This was her plan all along! I knew she must have some ulterior motive. Miss Feel-Bad-For-Me-and-My-Terrible-Childhood. She was baiting me, and I, like some dumb lobster, walked right into the trap.

Nice one, Dawn.

I screw up my face. "Ew," I say. "When I said I wanted to date people, I meant *people,* not moronic losers with superiority complexes."

"Dawn, you shouldn't talk that way," Mom scolds. "Besides, didn't you just say you weren't ready to settle down?" she asks, giving me a pointed look as she throws my words back in my face. Gotta give her props, she's planned this one well. "So why not date a few people? See who you like."

"I already know who I like. I like Sean. I detest Brent. In fact, I think Brent is hideous."

"But you and he have been friends since your country-club playpen days," my mother says, looking extremely disappointed. "And he's such a nice boy. Going to Yale next year, studying to be a lawyer."

"Yeah, but—"

"One date, Dawn. That's all I ask. If you don't like him,

you never have to see him again. But go with an open mind. Maybe you'll actually have fun."

"Uh, yeah. Probably as much fun as having my nose hairs plucked out one by one, I'm sure."

My mother frowns for a moment, then recovers. "Well, I'm certainly not going to force you to go, but I'd think you'd want to take advantage of getting out of the house for a night. . . ."

Man, she's thought of everything.

Suddenly, I see the total advantage of going on this date. Specifically, they'll have to give me back my cell phone—in case of emergency, you know. And if I have my cell phone, I can call Sean. Sure, I can't call Sean while Brent's right next to me, but Smarmy Little Rich Boy can't come into the ladies' room.

I take a deep breath. "Okay, Mom. I'll do it. One date."

My mom claps her hands together. She thinks she's won. Heh. Little does she know.

"Great, darling," she says. "You won't be sorry. Now let's go find you something to wear."

Chapter Nineteen

The doorbell rings promptly at six P.M. I can hear my parents rush to the door to greet the guy they've pimped me out to. Brent Baker the Third. Aka Golden Boy. Aka King Moron.

Reluctantly, I head downstairs.

"Hello, Mr. and Mrs. Miller," he says in his best Eddie Haskell from *Leave it to Beaver* voice. He looks up and sees me. "Dawn, you're looking very beautiful tonight. Not that," he adds, flashing a cheesy grin to The Evil Ones, "you don't always look lovely, of course."

Yeah, you look like your typical slimy self as well, I want to say, but hold my tongue. Must play along. I have a higher purpose here.

The way my parents are staring adoringly at Brent makes my stomach turn. How can they be so fooled by his obvious pandering? He's so cheesy I feel the sudden urge for crackers.

"Hi, Brent," I say. "What's up?"

My mother shoots me a look. Evidently "what's up" isn't proper date convo. But whatever. Like I give a care.

The only reason I agreed to this was so I can phone Sean. So any dreams she may have of a white wedding and a Vera Wang dress and fancy ivory invitations with bows that say "The Millers and the Bakers invite you to join them for a joyous event" can be tossed out the window now.

"Ooh, Richard, we should get the camera," my mom suggests.

Even Brent looks uncomfortable at that suggestion. Heh. "Actually, we have to get going," he says. "Reservations at the club for seven-thirty. And you know how Johan hates when people are late for their reservations." He winks at my dad.

Ew. We're going to the country club? I freaking hate that place. It's so snobby and formal and pretentious. The food sucks, too. All gourmet, with these tiny miniscule portions. Give me a burger and fries any day of the week.

"Oh we know that, all right," Dad agrees, slapping Brent on the back. *Gross.* "Okay, you kids go have fun now. Dawn, just give us a call if you're going to be out past eleven."

Wow. He's even going to let me break curfew, all in the name of Brent Baker the Third. What do they see in this guy? Just 'cause he comes from a wealthy family doesn't mean he's God's Gift to Teens. I mean, I'd have had to sell my soul to the devil before Mr. Curfew allowed me to stay out late. Though I guess, in a way, that's exactly what I've done.

"Okay," I say, throwing him a big smile. "Can I have my phone then? I mean," I say in my most casual voice, "in case I have to call, you know."

"Oh yeah, your phone. Good idea." Dad walks over to the closet and pulls my precious cell from a top-shelf box. Aha, that's where he stashed it. I've been looking everywhere. "Here you go."

Woot! My plan worked. I feel major elation as my fingers wrap around the receiver, its plastic frame more precious to me than gold.

"Okay, let's go," I say, stuffing the phone in my purse and opening the front door. Don't want to stick around in case he changes his mind. Besides, the sooner we leave, the sooner I can speak to Sean. He's going to be so psyched when he hears from me.

We head outside and into Brent's Mercedes. He opens the door for me, and I slip into the leather seat. It is a very nice car, I grudgingly admit. Too bad its driver is such a tool.

"Cool wheels," I say as Brent gets in the driver's seat. I have a feeling I'm going to have a hard time coming up with conversation tonight.

"Yeah. It's all right," Brent agrees. "It's just the SL500. I mean, I wanted to get the SL65, but the old man had the nerve to tell me it was too expensive. Puh-leze, right? I mean, we all know the stingy bastard could afford it."

Aww. He had to give up his dreams and settle for the hundred-thousand-dollar car instead of the two-hundred-thousand-dollar car. Sad story. Breaks my heart, really.

Brett prattles on, though. "So I said to him, 'Dad, the SL65 has twin-turbocharged V-12 engines. I mean, talk about massive power. This old thing only has a V-8.' And he says to me, 'Well, Brent, do you really need twin-turbocharged V-12 to get to school?' And I say, 'Dad, with the time it takes me to do my hair every morning, a car with twin-turbocharged V-12 engines would definitely come in handy. I get to school on time. I learn more. I get into Yale. I mean really, the thing is an investment in my future.' So he says, 'How about we get you the SL500 and then we bring it down to the dealership and we get it modified to be faster?' And so we did and we souped it up with a—"

Wow. I didn't realize it was physically possible to be so bored. Brent continues his Mercedes monologue all the way to the club. And I nod and say, "uh-huh," in a few choice places. This guy doesn't need a live date. He'd do perfectly fine with a blow-up doll.

We enter the club and the maitre d' seats us at a candlelit window table. Several of our parents' friends approach to say hi, looking more than delighted to see the two of us together. I catch a glimpse of Ashley #2 sitting at a table across the room. When she sees me with her beloved Brent, she gives me a dirty look and whispers something to her parents. Heh. Well, at least some good has come out of the otherwise lame-o date.

"Can I get you something to drink?"

I look up at the waiter and am about to ask for a Diet Coke, when Brent butts in.

"We'll have a bottle of your second-best champagne," he says. He glances over at me with another slimy grin. "We're celebrating tonight."

Uh, we are?

I wait for the waiter to ask for ID, to nip Brent's plan in

the bud, but he doesn't. He simply nods and retreats to get our bubbly. Oh-oh.

"We can't drink," I hiss at him after the waiter leaves. "I'm fifteen. You're seventeen."

Brent looks bored. "Grow up, Dawn," he says haughtily. "In Europe, kids can drink when they're twelve."

"But we're in Massachusetts!"

"Details, details." He waves his hand dismissively. "The guy served us, didn't he? That's all that matters."

I slump in my chair. You know, half of me thinks I *should* take a drink. Or twelve. In fact, I should get absolutely trashed and then wake up my parents when I get home. Maybe then they'd see Brent wasn't such a good guy after all.

But no. I want to keep a clear head so I can talk to Sean. Sean, who is straight edge and doesn't drink a drop. He'd be mad if I phoned him all inebriated.

"Will you excuse me a moment?" I ask in my sweetest voice. "Need to go to the ladies'."

"Sure. Whatever." Brent doesn't look up from his menu. "I'll order for you."

Of course you will.

I slip out of my chair and force myself not to run to the bathroom. The club has one of those bathrooms where there's a little sitting room with couches, so it's the perfect place to make my call. I'm so excited my hands are actually shaking. In a few brief moments, I'll be connected to my true love over the cellular airwaves. Did I mention how much I adore modern technology?

When I enter the bathroom, however, I notice feet

under several stalls. And I'm a little nervous that they could belong to friends of my parents. Or maybe Ashley #2. Someone who will tell on me for making an illicit phone call to my love while on a date with someone else. And I so don't want to get grounded for another two months.

Well, that blows. I guess I can wait 'til they leave, though that wastes precious talking time. Or, I suddenly realize, I can text him!

I sit down on one of the couches, pull out my phone and start typing. Sure, it's not as intimate as a phone call and I won't get to hear his sweet voice, but it's still one-on-one conversation with Sean. And right now, I'll take what I can get!

>*Hi Sean. Miss U!*

I hold my breath, hoping he's around and has his phone on him. That would really suck if he went out and left it at home or something, after all the trouble I've gone through.

>*Hi Dawn!!!*

Yay! He's there. I hug the cell to my chest for a moment, rejoicing in his virtual presence.

>*How R U?*

>*Good. R U off grounding?*

>*No. But I got a night off.*

How am I going to explain the whole date thing in text speech? It takes so long to type anything.

>*Where R U? Can I come see you?*

>*Ur never goin 2 believe this. But E.O.s forced me to go on a date with this loser guy.*

I hold my breath, waiting for his reply.

>*????*

>*WAIT! Don't freak. I only agreed coz I could call u.*

>*Ah. K. For a sec thought I should worry.*☺

I smile and tuck my legs under my bottom. He was jealous. Jealous of Brent. Aww. He's so adorable.

>*No need 2 worry. My heart belongs 2 U.*

> *:-) I luv u2.*

ARGHHH!!!!! I kiss my phone, prompting one of the old ladies exiting the bathroom to give me a weird look. But I so don't care. Sean loves me. He LOVES me.

Oh. I should probably not leave the poor guy hanging.

>*I wish I could come see u.*

>*Me too. I'd give u a big hug & kiss.*

>*I'd like that. V. much.*

We text a few more lines. Then I tell him I have to go, but I'll text him in a little bit. I can always make another trip to the bathroom while waiting for dessert or something.

I head back to the table, sure I'm still glowing from the exchange. Brent has already broken into the champagne and appears a little tipsy, which worries me. I don't want him driving me home drunk.

"Hey, Dawn, you missed it," he says as I sit down. "You know how I said I wanted their second-best champagne? Well, the loser brought us their fourth best. Like, thinking *I* wouldn't know the difference, I'm sure. So I said to him, do you know who my father is? And he says . . ."

I yawn. I can't help it. Luckily or unluckily, depending on your view, Brent doesn't catch it. He's too busy relating the tale of the evil waiter, who he triumphantly vanquished with his extensive knowledge of champagne vintages. Fascinating stuff, I'll tell you what.

Our meals come. Brent ordered me shrimp scampi, which I'm allergic to. I mention this, but he doesn't acknowledge me. He's too busy complaining about his own filet mignon, sending it back twice, complaining about the cut of the meat and then about its temperature. Then demanding to see the chef so he can berate him publicly. (With another reminder of just who his father is, in case the waiter forgot the first three times he told him.) Okay, this is gross, but I hope the chef hocks a big loogie in his mashed potatoes. It would totally serve him right.

Brent starts pouring himself a third glass of champagne and that's when I have to break into his monologue.

"Dude," I say, grabbing his hand. "You've got to drive me home. I'd appreciate it if you could do it soberly."

He looks sulky, but takes his hand off the bottle. "You know, I had a feeling you'd be this uptight, Dawn," he says. "You're such a stuck-up little snob at school."

Ni-ice! Great way to talk to one's date. I'm about to snark off a reply, when my purse buzzes by my feet. I reach down to retrieve my phone and read the text message from my lap.

>*How's the date?*

>*Sux.*

Brent's reheated meal shows up at that moment and he needs to come up with some other reason to yell at the waiter, so I'm able to text a few more messages to Sean, feeling a little like James Bond. There's something very intimate and sexy about sitting here, texting my true love, while my pseudo date sits across from me being a jerk-off. Very Romeo and Juliet, the next generation. In fact, I bet if those star-crossed lovers had text messaging back then, Juliet could have totally let Romeo in on her whole fake poison/death plan and then he wouldn't have had to kill himself over her. Would have made for a much happier ending.

Amazingly, the never-ending dinner from hell does finally end. Brent pays with his daddy's platinum card and we head out of the club. Thank goodness. Now I can go home and maybe my parents will forget about taking my phone back and Sean and I can text well into the night. Maybe we can even talk on the phone. After all, my bedroom is miles away from The Evil Ones' own chamber of horror. And our walls are pretty darn soundproof.

I look up. Where are we? Uh, wait a second.

"Where are we going?" I ask, as Brent turns off the main road. The main road that leads back to my house and back to my room. The main road that will bring us to the end of our miserable date and me closer to the time when I can start texting Sean again.

"Just for a drive," Brent says with a shrug.

Um, no thanks. I want to get home. To Sean. This date has already lasted ten thousand years too long.

"I'm, um, actually kind of tired." I fake a yawn. "Can you maybe just drop me off at home?"

"Just a little drive," Brent insists. "Then I'll take you home. It's a nice night."

Nice night, my butt. It doesn't take a linguist to translate guy talk.

"Besides, there's this cool place I want to show you."

Oh, huh! Let me guess. Could this "place" possibly, maybe, coincidentally be Lookout Point, by chance? OMG, he's so obvious, it's pathetic.

Lookout Point, as its name suggests, is the top of the hill above our East Oaks subdivision. It looks out over the entire city. On the plus side, it's very beautiful at night, with all the sparkling town lights. On the minus side, it's a well-known make-out place for teens.

And if Brent thinks I'm going to make out with him tonight, I've got a great bridge in Brooklyn I'd like to sell him!

But sure enough, he turns onto the windy road that leads up the hill to Lookout Point. It's foggy out and the car headlights do little to slice through the darkness. Kinda creepy, actually.

"Brent, I'd really like to go home." I try again, starting to get a little nervous. I should have never gotten into the car with him after he'd been drinking.

"Stop being such a freaking baby, Dawn," he admonishes, stepping on the gas and picking up speed.

It's at that point my heart starts pounding. He's not going to listen to me. What if when we get to the top he wants to . . . ?

No, I tell myself. He's my parents' friend's son. He's well educated and has been brought up with morals and manners. He wouldn't dare.

Would he?

"Please, Brent," I cry, knowing I sound scared and desperate and hating that I do. "Take me home."

He doesn't answer. Just keeps driving.

My hands shaking, I reach down to grab my purse. I glance over at Brent. His eyes are still glued to the road.

Pretending to rummage around inside for lipstick or something, I pull out my phone, set it on my lap, and text Sean.

>*Help. Lookout Point. Scared. Plz come.*

But will he be able to get here in time? He lives across town and we're almost to the top of the hill.

I text one more line.

>*Hurry!*

No answer. He probably walked away from his phone. Or went to bed. Great. I'm so screwed.

We reach the top of the hill and Brent puts the car into park. I look around, hoping some other lovelorn teens will be up here to provide assistance. But the place is deserted.

Brent does the not-so-subtle yawn and stretch and put his arm around my shoulder thing. I shrug away.

"What's your problem?" he asks grouchily.

"What's yours?" I retort. "I told you I wanted to go home."

"What's that?" His eyes fall on the phone in my lap. "Who are you calling?"

"No one."

"Good. Then you won't mind if I take that," he says, grabbing the phone and throwing it out the window.

"Hey! What did you do that for?"

"You know, Dawn," he says, his words slurring a bit. "You really need to lighten up."

"Lighten up? You just threw my freaking cell phone out the window!" I cry. "I'm going to go get it."

As my fingers fumble for the door handle, he reaches over and clicks the locking mechanism on his side, effectively thwarting my escape plan.

"Childproof locks." He laughs. "Gotta love it."

OMG! OMG! Now my heart is slamming against my ribcage with the rapid tempo of hardcore techno. I'm trapped. I have no phone. What if he tries to . . . ?

If only my parents could see me now. They'd be so sorry they made me go out with this so-called nice boy. A good family doesn't mean crap when you're drunk in a car on Lookout Point.

Brent reaches over and traces my cheek with a finger. I swallow hard, fear and adrenaline coursing through my veins. I don't know what to do. I stare straight ahead. I can see my house from here. If I kicked him where it counts, would I be able to climb over to his side of the car and unlock the door? Then I could run down the hill and make it home. But the cliff is really steep and it's pitch dark up here. I'd probably fall and break an ankle. Though that might still be better than the alternative. . . .

Brent leans in for the kill. Or in this case, the kiss. His alcoholic onion breath nauseates me as he smooshes his lips against mine. I get none of the butterflies that flutter through my insides when Sean kisses me. Instead I get angry wasps stinging my stomach with panic.

"Stop it!" I cry. But my open mouth only gives him the opportunity to stick his tongue down my throat. His hands grip my forearms so I can't pull away.

This is bad. Really, really bad. I knew Brent was a slime-ball, but I had no idea he'd go this far.

Please, Sean. Hurry!

I know in my heart that even if Sean did get my message, he won't make it in time. He's too far away. On the other side of town. I'm on my own, and I have to do something.

I force myself to relax under Brent's grip, then lean against the passenger-side door, allowing him to crawl on top of me. Then, when he's in position, I lift up my knee and slam it into his groin as hard as I can. At the same time, I bite down on his tongue.

"Ye-ow!" he cries, in an almost inhuman sound of pain. He tumbles backwards, clutching his privates with one hand and his tongue with the other. I think I actually made him bleed. "You bitch!"

But I don't wait to hear any more of his terms of endearment. I push past him, reach for the locking mechanism, and fall out of the car, stumbling as my foot catches on the door and slamming into the ground. A stab of pain shoots through me as my wrist breaks my fall onto the concrete.

Suddenly headlights cut through the fog. I jump to my feet, waving at them with my unhurt hand. Desperately hoping they're friend and not foe.

And then I recognize the car.

The Evil Ones.

And I've never been so happy to see them in my life.

"Help!" I scream, as loud as I can.

My dad leaps out of the driver's seat and drags the still-moaning Brent out of the car. Dad slams him against the hood, his hand against his neck.

"What the hell do you think you're doing with my daughter?" he demands in the most furious tone ever. Wow, I never realized my stodgy old dad kind of resembles a superhero at times.

My mom comes straight to me, wrapping her thin arms around my trembling body and leading me to the car.

"Are you okay, sweetie?" she asks, her voice laced with worry.

I motion to my wrist. It's throbbing like nobody's business. "I think it might be broken."

She takes my wrist gently in her hands, pressing cool fingers up and down the bone, all the while looking like she's going to cry.

"I'm so sorry, Dawn," she whispers. "This is all our fault."

Well, sort of. But even I know this isn't how they planned the night to go, so I guess can forgive them. "You didn't know what Brent was like," I say with a shrug, wincing as a new lightning bolt of pain snakes up my arm. "I didn't even know it."

"How dare you mess with my daughter?" I glance over to where Dad is still unleashing his fury on Brent, who, amusingly enough, looks as if he's going to pee his pants. Ha! Serves him right. "Have you been drinking?"

"No, sir, we were just goofing around and . . ."

"Sarah, call the cops," Dad yells over to my mother.

Brent's eyes bulge out in fright. "You can't do that! Think of what will happen to my dad—your friend—if it gets in the papers. And if Yale finds out . . ."

"You should have thought about that before you laid a hand on my daughter!"

Yeah! You tell him, Dad!

Wow. I've never seen my father so forceful and angry. Again it totally reminds me of Clark Kent turning into

Superman. Who knew he had it in him? I'm actually rather proud of the guy at this point.

I want to watch Dad torture Brent some more, but my mother insists on leading me to the car after she makes the call to the police. I sit in the front seat, shivering in my thin dress, and she blasts the heat while we wait for the cops to show up.

"How'd you find me?" I ask, my teeth still chattering, more out of nerves than chill.

My mom smiles. "Your friend Sean called."

Okay. Total jaw-dropping time. "He did?"

"Yes." Mom nods. "He said you were in trouble and he couldn't reach you in time, but thought since we were closer we could."

"And you believed him?"

Mom looks at me strangely. "Of course, Dawn. Why wouldn't we?"

Why wouldn't they, indeed. Well, for one, I would have assumed they'd think he was trying some trick. Seeing as he's a "crackhead" in their eyes. But when push came to shove, they swallowed their pride, believed his story, and came to my rescue, no questions asked. You know, for Evil Ones, they're pretty noble right about now. Maybe I should rethink the nickname. The Brave Souls Who Rescued Me from Certain Death, perhaps? Kinda has a ring to it.

"Thank you," I say. "I didn't know what I was going to do."

My mother looks pained. "I feel so terrible for forcing you into this, Dawn. You didn't want to go. You told me he wasn't a good boy, but I refused to believe it." She runs a hand through her graying black hair. "It's just that he comes from such a nice family. . . ."

"Character isn't based on income, Mom," I remind her. "And you can't judge a boy by his cover."

She turns and looks at me, a slight smile playing at the corners of her mouth. "When did you become so wise?" she asks. "You've grown up and I haven't noticed, have I?"

I nod, feeling tears prick at the corners of my eyes. "I guess so."

She leans in and pulls me into a gentle hug, careful of my wrist. "I know we haven't been the best parents," she says, her voice choking. "But we always tried to do what was best for you. Even though it probably didn't seem like it at the time. I hope you know we only did what we did because we love you so very much."

"I know, Mom. And you're really not that bad," I say with a giggle. "In fact, I wouldn't want anyone else."

The police show up then, sirens blaring, lights flashing, effectively drowning out any more sappy mom/daughter convo. Dad turns Brent over to them and it's handcuffing time for the drunk frat-boy wannabe.

After giving them my statement, we drive down the hill to the emergency room, where they set my arm. Turns out my wrist is broken in two places. Damn Brent. But he's gonna get his. I hope he has to share his jail cell with some big, scary-looking, lonely inmate.

"So this Sean who called us," my dad says on the way home. "Is he the boy from downtown?"

"Yes," I say, nursing my arm. The cast is already itchy. "He's the crackhead you grounded me over seeing."

"Can I assume we're being sarcastic with the term crackhead?"

"Uh, yeah, great that you noted it."

Dad glances in the rearview mirror, his eyes meeting mine. "How come you've never introduced us?"

I bow my head. "Because I was afraid you would forbid me to see him."

"That's what concerned me to begin with. Why would you think that? What's so bad about him that you would think we wouldn't want you dating him?"

"Nothing. Just . . ." I shrug. "He's poor. Real poor."

"So?"

I look up. "So you want me to date someone with a lot of money. Someone like Brent."

"I want you to date someone you like," Dad says. "Someone who will be nice to you and treat you with the respect you deserve. Someone who will worship the ground you walk on and realize what a gem you are." He pulls up to a stoplight and turns around to face me. "There are no minimum income requirements on your dates, Dawn. And there never were."

"Really?" I burst out into happy tears. "So I can start dating Sean again?"

The light turns green and my dad steps on the gas. "Well, you're not officially supposed to start dating 'til you're sixteen, but that's only a few weeks away." He glances over at Mom, who smiles back at him. "I guess we could make an exception. But we want to meet him first, of course."

I nod excitedly, my wildest dreams coming true. I can't believe it. I really can't believe it. "Okay. When do you want to meet him?"

"How about tomorrow?" Mom asks. "We could have dinner."

"Aghh!" I give an excited squeal. "Really? Tomorrow? I can see Sean tomorrow?"

I feel like I should be singing the Orphan Annie song.

Tomorrow, Tomorrow, I'll see Sean, tomorrow. He's only a day away!

This is so great. I'm sure once they meet Sean, give him a real chance, they're going to love him.

Love him like I already do.

Chapter Twenty

I'm nervous and pacing up and down my room as I wait for six P.M. I've changed my clothes three times already and that's no easy feat with a broken wrist. I want to look perfect. I want this night to be perfect. I want my parents (I've retired the name The Evil Ones, btw) to think Sean's perfect. Or at least, perfect for me.

The doorbell rings and I nearly jump out of my skin.

I rush downstairs, but I'm not fast enough to beat Mom and Dad to the door. I notice they too have dressed nicely for dinner. Dad in a black professor turtleneck and my mom a brightly colored Pucci dress.

I stand on the landing, holding my breath as they open the door. I'm suddenly worried for some reason that Sean will show up in his grungy skater clothes. Then I scold myself. Who cares what he wears? My parents need to accept him for who he is, not how he dresses. Isn't that, like, the whole Lesson with a capital "L" they've supposedly learned from all this?

Still, all that said, I have to admit I'm more than a little relieved when the open door reveals Sean in a navy blue suit and tie. It's a little too big for him around the shoulders, like it belonged to someone else at one point, but he looks yummy in it all the same. His hair is gelled back and he's freshly shaven. Delish! I want to jump his bones and kiss him senseless, but I restrain myself. It's probably not the move that would get him on the immediate good side of the 'rents.

"Hi, I'm Richard, and this is my wife, Sarah," my dad introduces, holding out a hand. "And," he adds with a grin, "I think you already know my daughter Dawn."

Sean smiles at my father and shakes his hand. A firm handshake, like my dad appreciates, not one of those limp fish ones. I can see my dad's approval. Score one for Sean, I mentally cheer.

"It's nice to meet you, sir," he says with a smile. (Sir? Okay, make that score two!) "And you too, Mrs. Miller," he adds, turning to my mom.

"Call me Sarah," Mom says.

Wow. She's letting him call her Sarah, that's huge! After all, Mom was a schoolteacher, so she's big on the whole Mrs. thing. She must like him already. I guess the whole saving me from the clutches of the evil Brent Baker the Third made a good first impression. But still, how cool is that?

I don't know what I was worried about. Sean's not a diamond in the rough at all. In fact, he'd be the most polished and gleaming gem in any jeweler's case. If we were at the country club, no one would give him a second glance.

This rocks!

"Hi, Sean," I say, descending the stairs.

"Dawn!" he greets me, his eyes shining, not hiding his adoration for me. I wonder if my parents notice the radiating love vibes between us. "I've missed you." He leans in and gives me a very respectable parents-are-in-the-room kiss on the cheek. Even the simple gesture sends those tingles to my toes. I can't wait 'til I get him alone so we can share a real kiss!

"Shall we eat?" Mom asks with a half-hidden smile to Dad.

We retire to the dining room. At first I'm a bit worried Sean might be weirded out by all the obnoxiously fancy furniture and rare artwork. But if he is, he hides it well. In fact, he waltzes through the house as if he were a prince, born to luxury.

Dad, Sean, and I take our seats at the table and my mother hustles around to get dinner served. She told me earlier she gave Magda the night off. I'm not sure if that was a random act of kindness or because she didn't want Sean to be freaked out by his neighbor serving him dinner, but hey, whatever works. It's also highly amusing to see Mom try to play waitress/cook. She drops at least three things on the floor and the mashed potatoes are beyond lumpy. But it's cool. At least she's making the effort.

Finally, when we're all served and Mom's seated, my dad starts in with his traditional game of Twenty Questions. Though this time, his interrogation is directed at Sean, not me. At least he doesn't have the guy hooked up to a lie detector machine like poor Ben Stiller in *Meet the Parents*.

"So, Sean, tell us about yourself," he says, starting out with an easy one.

Sean swallows his bite of food before speaking. Good one. Mom hates the talking-with-your-mouth-full thing I always do.

"Well, I'm seventeen years old. I'm a senior at Woodbury," he begins.

Now that I'm closer to him, I can see he is a little nervous. I guess, who wouldn't be? I mean, my dad is pretty darn intimidating. Sean's hiding it well, though.

"Where are you going to college next year?" my dad asks.

My heart sinks. So much for warm-up questions. I remember all too well Sean saying he probably can't afford to go to college. And it was a pretty sore subject, too, if I remember right. But if he says he's not going to college, my dad's going to freak out and think Sean's some loser with no future. 'Cause as we all know, my dad's biggest hang-up is the college thing.

"You know, college isn't really for everyone—" I start to say, ready to jump in and save Sean in any way possible.

"Harvard," Sean says.

"—I mean, look at Bill Gates. He's a college drop . . ." I trail off, turning to look at Sean, open-mouthed.

Did he just say Harvard? He didn't just say Harvard! Did he?

I glance over at my dad, whose eyes are currently sparkling brighter than any Christmas lights. I guess I must have heard right. But how can Sean be going to Harvard? Is he lying just to impress my dad? I hope not, 'cause that would be so easy for him to check up on and I know my dad well enough to know he will have a ton of follow-up questions to this news of the century.

"Really?" My dad asks, not disappointing. "You know, I went to Harvard."

"Yes, Dawn mentioned that," Sean says, smiling at me. He doesn't look like he's lying. But, how . . . ? I'm so confused.

"What are you studying there?"

"Computer science, most likely."

My dad is beaming at him like he's found his long-lost son. "Well, they've got a great program there. Actually, all their programs are great. I keep trying to tell Dawn that." He motions his head to me with a conspiratorial look toward Sean. "But she doesn't want to go."

Sean shrugs. "Well it's not for everyone, for sure. But it's always been my number-one choice."

"Well, if you end up pledging a fraternity . . ."

My dad spends pretty much the rest of the meal discussing Harvard with Sean. I glance over at Mom, who winks at me. She knows this couldn't be going better if we'd planned it.

But Sean going to Harvard? I'm so confused.

After dinner, my dad suggests Sean and I go for a walk. Which of course I'm delighted to do, to get some alone time with him. And I've got a billion questions buzzing in my brain that I'm dying to ask him.

We step outside into the crisp night air and walk down the driveway to the street. Once we're out of possible parental view, Sean pulls me behind a tree and kisses me.

Ah, how I've missed this. His hot lips on mine, his peppermint breath. I relax into the kiss, feeling more alive and happy than I have in weeks. God, I love him.

But wait, I have questions!

I pull away. "So what's the deal with all that Harvard stuff?" I ask. "You never said you were going to Harvard. Did you make that up to get my dad to like you?"

He laughs and kisses me again. "Of course not, silly," he says. "Why would I do that? You really have a bad opinion of me, don't you?"

"No," I say defensively, "but you never told me you were going to Harvard."

"You've been grounded a long time, girl," he reminds me. "I got my acceptance letter a week ago. I've been dying to tell you, actually."

"Wow!" I cry, throwing my arms around him in a celebratory hug. "That's so awesome."

"Yeah. I was completely stoked." He hugs me back, then leans against the tree's trunk, staring at the ground. "Of course, I didn't want to say this in front of your dad, but I'm still not positive I can go."

"Oh?" My heart sinks a little. I knew it was too good to be true.

"Yeah. 'Cause of the money, you know. I mean, I was lucky—they were real generous in the financial-aid package. But I've still gotta come up with cash for books and stuff. Those technology books can cost over a hundred bucks each."

"Ugh."

"Yeah." He nods. "Ugh."

"You don't look too worried, though."

He shrugs. "Well, remember that skating competition I told you about?"

"Yeah." It seems a lifetime ago that we sat in the chill-out room at the rave, discussing our dreams. The first night we kissed. So much has happened since.

"Well, it's next week. And if I can win that, the scholarship money they're giving away will more than cover my books. Actually, it'd probably get me my own laptop as well."

"Oh cool!" I exclaim, hope regained. "You'll totally win. I know you will."

He grins. "Thanks for the vote of confidence. I'm not quite as sure as you are, but hey, I'm going to give it my best shot, right?"

"And I'll be there to cheer you on!"

He smiles and leans in to kiss me softly on the mouth. I swear, even if we end up old and gray and in matching rocking chairs on our front porch, I'll never lose that tingly feeling his kisses evoke.

"I wouldn't have it any other way."

Epilogue

"Ooh, the program says Sean's up next after this guy," I note, looking up from the leaflet and scanning the top of the half-pipe for some sign of my boyfriend. Don't see him yet.

"About freaking time!" Starr exclaims, shifting in her uncomfortable bleacher seat. "We've been here like hours. Who knew there were so many skaters in Massachusetts?"

Eddie laughs. "And these are just the ones good enough to qualify for regionals. Doesn't even count poor slobs like me."

"Aww, is baby feeling left out?" Starr coos, putting an arm around Eddie and kissing him on the cheek. Since Starr's gotten off groundation, she and her mohawked boyfriend have been completely inseparable.

"Nah, I know the Seanster will do well to represent our 'hood." Eddie says, making funny fake gangsta hand signals. We crack up.

Starr cups her mouth with her hands. "Fall, you loser!" she cries to the guy currently up on the pipe. "You suck!"

I elbow her in the ribs, laughing. "That's not very nice!"

"Hey, we need Sean to have every advantage possible," she says, defending her other-skater sabotage. She cups her mouth again. "Why don't you take up basket-weaving, you loser?"

It's a beautiful Sunday, and Starr, Eddie, and I are all hanging out in the grandstands of Woodbury High stadium, which has been transformed into a skate park for the day. The sun warms the top of my head and I've never felt so happy. In fact, I feel like I've won the life lottery.

When Sean left that night after dinner with my parents, they were immediately all over me, telling me how much they loved him. How impressed they were by him. How I couldn't have picked a better guy to be my first boyfriend. Sooo cool.

And then we had a long talk. They asked me what I wanted to do with my life and actually—get this!— listened to my answer. I told them I couldn't deal with the overscheduling and extra-extracurricular activities and they said I could plan my own schedule from now on, as long as I continued to do well in school.

So I've ditched Japanese, crew, and yearbook. And kept on ballet and gymnastics. (Don't want to turn into a slug, after all!) And I joined the school paper so I could become a better writer.

Speaking of which! My poem got selected for *Faces*. No, not just selected—I won first place! Next month I'll be the featured selection for the literary journal. I even get mentioned on the cover! And because of my parents' change of heart, I don't even have to use a pen name. My real name, Dawn Ashley Miller, will appear next to my poem for everyone to see.

Okay, so it's only a regional literary magazine, not an Oprah Book Club selection, but it's still extremely satisfying. And besides, today *Faces*, tomorrow the world, right?

My dad even went so far as to say he's proud of me. In fact, he promised to stop calling my poems "little limericks" from now on and that he'd take my writing dreams seriously. Sure, he's still not keen on the whole poetry-as-a-career-choice thing, but he said if I were to major in English, at least I'd have something like teaching to fall back on.

So all in all, life is good for Dawn. Very good.

Sure, not everything's perfect. I'm still a bit of a social reject at school. But I don't care. I have my friends. Sean, Eddie, Starr. Sophie and Stuart. Friends who really care about me for who I am and not where I shop. Who will stand by me and encourage me to follow my dreams and support me in whatever I do.

Brent Baker the Third's dad used all his family connections to get the kid out of jail time. But he couldn't get him off many, many hours of community service. We like to go downtown some Saturdays and watch Abercrombie Boy pick garbage off the sidewalks. I'm sure it'll look great on his college application.

"There he is!" Starr squeaks, pointing up to the left half of the ramp. I follow her hand to see Sean, standing at the top, looking tall and sexy in his baggy skater clothes. My heart flutters with love and anticipation. I think I'm more nervous than he is! I want him to win so badly. 'Cause it's his dream. And I, for one, know how important dreams are.

"Look how cute that guy is," I hear a girl say to my right. I glance over. An eighth-grade Barbie with braids in her hair is pointing at Sean.

"Mmm. He's a wicked good skater, too," her friend says. "I saw him in the qualifying round."

"With that bod, I wouldn't care if he totally sucked," Barbie says with a giggle. "I'd be his skater girl any day."

I smile, feeling old and wise and oh-so cool. "Sorry, that position's taken," I say.

"Is he your boyfriend? He's so awesome!" the girl says, looking at me like I'm Lindsay Lohan or some other Hollywood star.

"Yes, he is," I agree, watching as Sean drops from the top of the ramp into a crouched position and traverses to the other side of the pipe. As he starts up the ramp, he straightens his legs and then takes flight, twisting his body and board in the air—and then hitting the ramp perfectly on the way back down. Then he skates up the other side to do it all over again.

My heart stops for a moment each time he goes for a trick. Each time praying he doesn't fall. Lose the competition that means so much to him. Or worse, get hurt.

But he's too good. He aces every trick—even the complicated ones—and when his time is up, he hops back onto the top of the pipe and raises his skateboard above his head in victory. He knows he's nailed it.

The crowd goes absolutely wild. Barbie and her friend leap up and cheer. Eddie and Starr hug each other in glee.

"Woot! Go, Sean!" I yell as loud as I can, my voice practically giving out after all my whooping. "I love you!"

He seems to hear me, even over the roar of the crowd, and flashes me a triumphant grin.

He doesn't have to wait for the judges to announce his scores. He knows he's won. He knows that at this moment, all his dreams have come true.

And so have mine.

A Bird,
a Bloke, and
a Boyfriend
Sally Odgers

A recipe for romance?

Take one bird. (That's Sarah, arm-wrestling champion extraordinaire.)

Add one bloke, who's known the bird forever. (That's A.J., who lives next door.)

Stir in one boyfriend—literally made to order. (That's Clay.)

Set the whole thing to rise in a tropical sun-soaked paradise called Pirates' Point, and what have you got?

That depends who you ask. Ask a simple question and you never get a straight answer from anyone....

Got Fangs?
Katie Maxwell

I used to think all I wanted was to have a normal life. You know, where I could be one of the crowd and blend in, so no one would know just how different I am. But now I'm stuck in the middle of Hungary with my mom, working for a traveling fair with psychics, magicians, and other really weird people, and somehow, blending in with this crowd doesn't look so good.

Fortunately, there's Benedikt. Yeah, he may be a vampire, but he has a motorcycle, and best of all, he doesn't think I'm the least bit freaky. So I'm supposed to redeem his soul—if his kisses are anything to go by, my new life may not be quite as bad as I imagined.

- -

Didn't want this book to end?

There's more waiting at **www.smoochya.com**:

Win FREE books and makeup!
Read excerpts from other books!
Chat with the authors!
Horoscopes!
Quizzes!
